iDEAD

and other short stories

WYATT TREMBLAY

Published by Raspberry Press

www.raspberrypress.ca

ISBN: 978-1-7780881-3-1

Cover photo and design by: Wyatt Tremblay

FOREWORD

I have always had a vivid imagination coupled with an equally vivid dream life. In my waking world, as a political cartoonist and a writer, my ability to imagine the outlandish and envision the impossible has given me endless pleasure and opportunity. In my sleeping world, my dreams are most often fully scripted stories, with a beginning, a middle, and an ending. I forget most of them when I awake, though I can be aware that something fantastic happened while much of me was comatose.

In this collection of short stories, written between 2003 and 2007, you'll find a collection of stories pulled from these two worlds. From a co-worker whose endless dialogue is an analog blog in the workplace to the sad idea of a completely human-less way to pass from life to death, to a disturbing encounter with a baby on a sidewalk, they all come from my imagination and my dreams. The stories may be varied, but they have a common theme, reflections on the joys, sorrows, and hopes of life.

INDEX

For my children, who gave me laughter and tears, and who grounded me in the real world.

1. ANALOG BLOG

JULES IS A DECENT ENOUGH PERSON. She is a substantial Nova Scotian, hailing from Halifax's red brick and shrubbery-lined suburbs. She is eager to please and generous to a fault, often supplying Tim Horton's donuts or home-baked fare to her fellow cubicle dwellers. As a graphic designer, she has a quick and creative mind, tackling challenging deadlines like a hulking linebacker. All this employability, however, is marred by one frustrating flaw. No, let's call it what it is, a maddening quirk, an aberration of character.

She is excessively garrulous.

I'm not exaggerating. She quite literally never stops talking. From the time she blasts, like a hurricane, into the office, to that final merciful second when she punches out, there is not one minute where I, or any of my fellow office workers, can enjoy a meaningful, reflective moment of silence. Oh, don't get me wrong, there is nothing inappropriate with chatting it up at the office, but there comes the point where one more excruciating tale about explosive diarrhea or the outrageous antics of Fritz, her Siamese cat, and I tend to lean alarmingly into the red zone of my insane-o-metre.

Wrapped in her thick East Coast accent, she voluminously occupies the cubicle next to mine along with two other designers whose deliberate monosyllabic responses unfortunately only provide her with a continuous opportunity to further pollute the atmosphere with a never-ending and mind-numbing monologue. As a result, I know more about the life of Jules Olivia Manson, and her cat, her mother, her twin sister (and also what a superb graphic designer her "Sis" is), her mailman, her grocer, her mechanic friend Steve, and Willie, the plumber, the guy she spends most Saturday nights with, and her hairdresser, her 'personal' trainer and aesthetician, and all sixteen of the neighbours in her apartment block, than I do about my own simple life.

There are, thank God, fifteen splendidly peaceful hours between the marks on the clock when I lurch out of the office in the evening and reluctantly when I have to sign in the next morning. Precious hours where I do not have to waste one more second of the best years of my life being forced by the sheer volume of her voice to listen to her free-flowing ramble. Unfortunately, this does mean Jules has lived these fifteen hours, and, according to her, she lives them quite largely. The events which occur during those hours she feels compelled to regurgitate the next day at work. She is the metaphorical unwanted mother of the nest, vomiting the most gratuitous drivel anyone could wish to inflict upon even their most hated enemy.

"Jerry," Alf interrupted my rant while nodding with genuine understanding and sympathy, "it's obvious. You're dealing with an analog blogger."

Alf works on the floor above mine in the television and web design department. He used to occupy a station in my cubicle until he was promoted. There is a position opening in his department and, as if you hadn't already guessed, I've applied (done everything but fall to my knees and beg) for the job. He and I are office friends. We meet for lunch in the cafeteria across the street and vent all our working woes upon each other. It's therapeutic, though it hasn't honestly done much help to me of late. We used to mix our office talk with discourses on golf, the continuous losing streak of the Ottawa Senators, or whatever action flick was exploding across the silver screen. Then, like some primordial Leviathan, Jules rose from the murky depths. Three months earlier, she joined the magazine ad-design team, promoted from the floor beneath mine where she worked—quite effectively, she has informed all within listening range on innumerable and insufferable occasions—designing retail flyers and ad banners for print media.

"Analog blogger?" I repeated.

Alf nodded as he tapped his lips thoughtfully with his fork, "It's like a blog, only instead of being digital, like on the Internet, it's right there in front of you, streaming from her mouth. She's an analog blog."

I chuckled. Jules Manson was a three-dimensional, non-virtual blog, heaving the routine details of her dull, ordinary life upon her office mates like a dog vomiting after gorging on a bag of dog food.

"Jerry, I can see the dark circles forming under your eyes. You are stressed out, man. Any ideas on what you're going to do?"

"I applied for that position," I mumbled, feeling not too hopeful.

Alf slowly shook his head and exhaled noisily, "Not good enough, my friend. It'll be at least three months. Do you think you can last that long?"

I stared at him and suddenly felt like leaping off the CN Tower—without a parachute.

Three months? Oh, God.

I taped the printout to Jules' monitor before she clocked on Monday morning. It read:

Miss Manson, we are happy to have you as part of the magazine ad design team of Foster and Pickles. You have shown excellent proficiency in your field. The design and layout you provided for the Wiggles Toy Store account were creative and refreshing in their originality. It is a pleasure to work with you. However, would it be possible for you to refrain from talking so often as some of us have found it difficult to remain focused on projects of our own? Thank you for your consideration in this matter, Your fellow employees.

There were no "fellow employees." I acted alone for the good of the whole. Pump her up, then let her down. That's what Alf had instructed me to do. The note was polite, wasn't it? Gentle, yet firm, without being offensive, right? Wouldn't any reasonably sane human being have grasped the import of my carefully scripted words?

The blast of fiery disapproval could be heard from the coffee room three cubicles away, and one could immediately feel the pall of tension descend upon the office as if the Angel of Death had suddenly made an appearance.

"Hah," she grunted.

"Hah!" She lobbed her verbal bomb again, the blast radius reaching explosively to consume the entire floor. "Which one of you neophytes wasted perfectly good and expensive printer paper on this ridiculous note?"

I cringed in my cubicle, the dragon's breath bearing down upon my neck. I could only imagine the terror my co-workers were facing behind the fabric and plastic partition that separated us. Someone mumbled from behind the wall. It might have been Millie; she doesn't say much. Well, she never needed to; Jules does all the talking.

"Well?" Jules bellowed.

Another mumbled reply.

"Ah well, prob'ly a joke, eh? Is it April Fools' Day or something? I don't talk too much, eh Millie? What's that? Speak up, honey. You gotta use those lips the good Lord gave you, huh? No? Not too loud? Didn't think so. Steve, now that guy talks like a freight train rumbling across a trestle bridge. Sweet merciful Minerva, he can talk nineteen to the dozen, that boy. Let me tell you, just last night the phone rings, my cell phone, eh—jingles the Charlie's Angels theme, eh—and I, like, answer it and it's Steve. Says he's bootin' a hot truck load of Chevy parts up to Windsor...."

And Jules was off like a thoroughbred ripping up the track in pursuit of the Triple Crown. It was unbelievable. I sagged in my chair and cried, sobbing bitterly but quietly in my cubicle. How could any living, breathing human being be so completely thick?

"Oh, jeez. That sucks," Alf offered by way of sympathy at lunch.

"Tell me about it; I nearly offed myself."

"So, she's still talking up a storm?"

"My ears are still ringing."

I sighed and took a deep swig of coffee. It was too hot, and I slammed the cup down, scalding Java sloping over my hand.

"Ah! I can't go on. I don't want to know anything more about her bowel movements or, dear God, her sex life."

"Well, there's always the promotion to look forward to," he stared off at nothing, "uh, only ninety-three days if you get it."

"Yeah, thanks. What? What do you mean 'if'?"

Alf shrugged.

"Has anyone referred you yet?"

"Referred me?"

He nodded, "Yeah, you're heading for the big times, man. You can apply for the job, but you must get at least three referrals from co-workers. It lets upper management know you're a team player and are qualified to do the job."

"Oh … oh!"

I collected nine signatures in three minutes. The hope in my fellow prisoners' eyes made me feel like a hero like I was Homer's Odysseus blinding the monstrous Cyclops. Okay, perhaps I'm being a trifle melodramatic, but for the first time in three months, there was the faintest glimmer of hope, of light at the end of the black, jabber-choked tunnel we had been trapped in.

I filled out an application for the job—the one I had so wanted, on the floor above in television and web-ad design. I expertly forged Jules' signature and hand-delivered the package to the personnel department. All I had to do, all we had to do, was sit it out for three months, like a hijacked airplane full of hostages on the hot tarmac of life waiting to be rescued. Ninety days and our analog blogger could blog somewhere else.

"You idiot. How could you do that to me?" Alf sputtered when I smugly informed him of what I had done.

"Oh," I mumbled, the glowing warmth of my self-satisfaction rapidly cooling. "I hadn't thought of that."

Getting rid of Jules had become an obsession for me. No one ever said that madness was girded in logic or common sense.

"I'm sorry."

"Sorry?" Alf slapped his forehead. "You've gotta undo this, Jerry."

"I don't think I can. She's already received a letter of confirmation."

"Oh, God. Oh, no."

"She blathered on about it for hours."

"Oh, God!"

"She says it's some kind of Mary, Jesus and Joseph miracle."

"Oh, God! How could you do this?"

"I'm sorry. I was desperate."

"I'm doomed."

Three months can feel like quite a long time—like an eternity, to be exact. By comparison, Dante was having a cheery Sunday afternoon picnic in the raging fires of Hell in the Inferno. It felt that way. Over the following painful weeks, Jules talked enough to fill several football stadiums with her pointless ramblings. I am now privy to her bra size, her waist and shoe sizes, how many hairs she removes from her eyebrows and upper lip on Sunday mornings, what an all-inclusive cell phone package she has, and what her favourite episode of American Idol was, and whom she hated the most on Survivor: Alaska, and, dear God, how much wind she can pass and for how long after an evening of "packing it in" at McNabb's Bar and Grill flaming hot chilli night.

I have stained a dozen shirt sleeves with my tears. I have downed more super-strength painkillers than I'm sure it is safe to consume. I have cracked more knuckles and beat my aching head with my fists more often than is wise, but, thank God, time marches relentlessly forward.

The sun rose, and the day arrived. Jules was given official notice that she was a successful candidate. We stifled our cheers and bought her a gift of semi-expensive chocolates, and a humorous card that we all signed with sweet lies about how we would miss her, and she, chatting ceaselessly until the end, packed up her personal effects, and moved upstairs. As the elevator doors slid shut, heads began to pop up behind cubicle walls like gophers emerging from their holes after a coyote had passed. The danger was gone. The sacred merciful sound of silence descended upon us all.

Of course, as the laws of the universe must dictate, for every action, there is an equal and opposite reaction. Jules' promotion left a vacancy in our department, and the cruellest of all cosmic jokes was played upon us. She has a twin sister, and I do mean twin. She is identical in every way. I'm serious. Jennifer, or Jen, or Jenny-bells, or Jen-tastic as she has taken to educating us, is a carbon copy of her sister's tragic and disturbing and noisy idiosyncrasy. Oddly enough, though Jules had chattered incessantly about her sister, she had never once mentioned that the graphic design company that employed her was indeed the same one we all worked at.

As fate continued to have its cruel way with us, the ludicrous irony of my situation caused Alf to break down into such spastic convulsions of laughter that he choked on a mouthful of a cheeseburger, jamming a clump of charbroiled beef, Romaine lettuce and kosher pickle thoroughly in his esophagus. To my horror, he suffocated to death despite numerous Heimlich maneuver attempts by a teenage waiter and an overwrought dental assistant. Unfortunately for her, I felt, they happened to be sitting next to us in the cafe.

In this fortuitous but bizarre twist, the tragic passing of my friend has created a position in his department. I am not applying for it. Instead, I am forging another signature on an application: Jennifer Manson.

Could you imagine those two in the same space? I'm almost positive the universe would collapse into the verbal black hole such a union these two analog bloggers would create.

Note: Analog Blog - This story is based on a dream where I was working with a colleague who seemed unaware of what was and wasn't appropriate to share in an office setting. After I told a friend about the dream, he came up with the phrase, analog blog. He felt it best described the person in my dream whose main topic of discussion was themselves. Their day-long verbal discourse was a non-digital blog of their life. The only way to 'unsubscribe' was to exit the building.

2. MOUNTAINS TO CLIMB

THERE WAS A SUDDEN LOUD BANG. I'm not exaggerating. It was sudden and loud, causing me to flinch and duck. I don't know why I ducked. It made little difference. Something hit me from above. It fell from the sky, glanced off the left side of my head, off my shoulder, and landed with a dull thud in the snow beside me.

It was a raven.

Singed, smouldering, and definitely dead.

It twitched once, and then the stench hit me: roasted flesh, burnt feathers, ozone. I looked up. The wretched creature had fried itself on an electrical transformer. Sparks were still sputtering at the top of the power pole like the last gasps of a spent Roman candle.

This was not how my day began.

It began like this: Shelley nudged me.

I rose triumphantly from the command chair of the USS Reliant, having just vanquished the Borg from my sector of space in a bloody but decisive battle. Shelley elbowed me again. I stumbled and fell as a surprise quantum torpedo attack rocked the ship. The Borg had returned.

"Mmm?"

"Honey, Adam's crying. It's your turn."

I picked myself up, waiting for the inertia dampers to cycle back on. The proximity-threat klaxon sounded. Red alert. Another hit. I grabbed the arm of the command chair to steady myself.

"Ow," Shelley hissed, pulling my hand from her thigh, "Wake up!"

"Mmm?"

The view screen rippled like a rock had been dropped into its fluidic depths, then exploded, showering the bridge with shards of flesh-piercing meta-glass. Needle-sized slivers slammed into my shoulder. I jerked away. Too late, I was down again.

"Alex."

Shelley pinched me in the arm.

"C'mon. Get up. He's been crying forever."

"Ensign," I muttered, "to your duty station."

"Excuse me?"

I threw the quilt back farther than I needed to. Shelley complained and grabbed a handful of bedding, drawing its warmth around her neck. The floor was cold.

Stupid Borg, they were constantly interfering, always assimilating, always insisting on galactic domination. I bounced off the hallway walls, tripping into Adam's room. He was standing with his arms outstretched, his face flushed and puffy from crying.

"Hey, my little Vulcan science officer, why the tears?"

His face split into a wide grin. He leapt into my hands as I pulled his little body to my chest, holding him until the sobs subsided. He was wet and hungry. I changed his diaper and gave him a warm bottle.

It was my turn?

How did this happen?

How did I get here? Standing in my son's bedroom, feeding and caring for someone so small and utterly dependent upon me? Wasn't I just that kid standing in my crib screaming for a parent? Didn't I just graduate from college?

I sank wearily into the rocking chair next to the crib and cradled my son, tilting the bottle so he could leach the last few drops from its plastic milk bag. His lips were puckered, sucking, but he was asleep. He was on automatic. I felt the same way, I guess. Foot to the accelerator, brake lines cut, barreling full-speed ahead. One day—and all too soon, I feared—I would be an old man—Bald, worn out, and married to a woman who had aged along with me. Of course, she would still have her hair. Some things just aren't fair, it seems.

Fear. That's what I was feeling—feeling trapped, too. Adam wasn't planned for. Shelley hadn't been in the cards, either. There were still mountains to climb, airplanes to jump out of, and universe-spanning empires to build.

Still, I was, holding this wonderful but needy little being in my arms. Somehow, all of this had just simply happened. No fanfare. No parade and no, "Look, Ma, I'm marching off to war." No dragon to slay and certainly no damsel to rescue. It hadn't taken much, either, to catch me. A look, a stolen glance, a smile, that body, the first nervous conversation, the first date, the second—and now, here I was, my head still caught in the spin cycle. Married, a child, a mortgage, a yard to mow, a car, and bills.

How did this happen?

The raven twitched one final time. Its eyes were sightless pits burst open from the surge of electricity that had coursed violently through its body. One fatal mistake, one careless step, and there it was. The end had come. No more mountains to climb, airplanes to jump out of, or universe-spanning empires to build. Just like that, it was over. Finis.

I nudged the bird with my boot and looked up at the smoking transformer. The power was probably out for a bunch of people on this block.

Adam reached a hand around, groping for my face from where he was securely strapped to my back in his child carrier.

"Mfp-ag-pf?" he asked.

I took his small mitten-covered hand in mine and squeezed his fingers.

"S'ok, Adam. He's just sleeping; he's taking a break from ruling the universe."

Yup, that's me, I realized. I was taking a break from building my universe-spanning kingdom of testosterone-laden adventures. Adam, Shelley, they were my mountain now, my wild jump from a nightmarish height, without a parachute, no less. They were my empire, unplanned and unexpected. They were just there before me, waiting for me, needing me.

I took one final look at the dead raven, shifted Adam's weight on my shoulders, and trudged on, heading for home, the mortgage, the yard, and Shelley—my universe.

It wasn't so bad.

I could be lying back there with my eyeballs burned to a crisp.

Note: The manner of the raven's death in Mountains to Climb is factual. I have witnessed this startling event. Perhaps the most unusual was the day a raven met its end on a transformer and fell to the ground beneath the pole. Within moments, over 30 ravens circled their fallen comrade, calling each other. This lasted for about five minutes, and then they, one by one, flew away. It was very strange.

3. TOUCHED

ALEX MCKENZIE WAS THE SORT OF MAN whose sheer, unnatural size made you pause and stare open-mouthed at him—though you didn't dare for long. If he felt your eyes upon him and returned your look, a cold shiver would play at the back of your neck, and you'd quickly realize that he could snap that neck if he so desired. Mick, or Mick the Crusher, as he was known on the street and among his friends—ones you might be hesitant to label as the friendly type—carried his impressive mass with an aggressive self-assurance that was partly encouraged by his gargantuan stature but mainly it was because he'd never encountered anyone larger or meaner. He'd been ducking his head through doorways since he was fourteen, about the same time he realized he'd found a particular, manic pleasure in breaking things.

His hands were the size of footballs, his feet size 18, and his shoulders and arms so massive he had clothing tailored to fit. More often than not, these were bought or stolen from a quaint little shop over on Fifty-seventh Street, run by a Jamaican immigrant named Mel. Mick revelled in his physical prowess and enjoyed making any and all feel uncomfortable with his imposing bulk. He never wasted an opportunity to employ it to obtain whatever his callous heart desired. So, it came as quite a surprise, not only to his petite girlfriend, his third in seven months, but also to his closest associates, when he was found late one night hunched over, halfway up Fifty-first Street, in a dark and garbage-strewn dead-end alley usually frequented by prostitutes and their clients. He was sobbing uncontrollably, like a frightened little child.

Officer Milton Twigge, who was summoned to the scene by an anonymous caller, found Mick in this pathetic and unbecoming condition. Twigge knew the hulking man personally from the many times he had arrested him. Well, as personal as one can get on the receiving end of Mick's signature lightning-fast right hook. It took Twigge, three other police officers, and two conscripted and disgruntled pedestrians to remove Mick from the alley. He kicked, sobbed terribly, hollered great unspeakable obscenities and cast anxious and, as one observer said, "terror-filled glances" toward the dark alley where he had been found.

When they finally managed to coerce his brutish weight into the paddy wagon, it was only then that he ceased thrashing like one who had seen the very face of the Grim Reaper himself. Even then, with the doors locked shut and the fume-spewing vehicle speeding off into the night, he cowered in the farthest, darkest corner of the wagon. Officer Twigge said later that it seemed as if Mick the Crusher was grateful to have had his meaty hands chained to his enormous feet.

A court-appointed psychiatrist labelled Mick as psychotic and suffering from an acute neurosis exacerbated by a disturbingly palpable fear of—well, they weren't quite sure what had frightened Mick, as he wasn't saying. He refused to say anything to anyone, not even to Macy, his girlfriend. Witnesses say they observed her hurried departure from the police station the following afternoon. There were rivers of tears pouring down her face. She packed her belongings the following day, her friends said and moved back to Moose Jaw to care for her ailing mother.

The cops, whom he had pummelled for a decade or more, called the loss of Mick's particular version of sanity, karma, an act of fortuitous, cosmic revenge. Shop owners and decent folk he had terrorized sighed great sighs of relief. His friends, acquaintances, and associates shook their heads in disbelief. His sudden bout of insanity was a loss to the kinship of criminals—well, for about a day and a half. A turf war erupted over who would replace Mick as the most brutal, most vicious thug to be called the undisputed "King of the Streets."

What of Mick? Something happened to the Crusher that night, something strange and mysterious. Some say he was touched in his head.

A year to the day after the incident, Mick was released from the psych ward of Belmont Hospital, and soon after that, he could be seen, in his trademark dark trench coat, wandering the impoverished streets of his old haunts. He was still the same outsized, imposing man he had always been. One might even feel that old tickle of fear at the back of the neck upon first glance, but something was decidedly different. He was smiling. Not that he hadn't smiled before, especially while crushing the arms or legs of one of his victims or while shoving the barrel of his favourite weapon, a nickel-plated Smith & Wesson .45, in the face of some poor, trembling store clerk. No, this smile was different. It was a happy thing, a joyous grin even. It was disturbing. His old friends saw this transformation and scratched their heads, wondering what odd scam the Crusher was up to and how much cash he was going to haul in. His many enemies peered cautiously at him as if they were about to meet the terrible old right hook. However, he would pass them all by, smiling and sometimes whistling.

To add to the confusion, the Crusher began doing very strange things. He took to picking up garbage, and, well, he did the unimaginable; he began helping people. He carried an elderly man in his arms, with a heavy bag of groceries, up three flights of stairs in an old ramshackle tenement building. He broke up a squabble between a warring gang of youths, taking their knives and clubs and giving them a basketball. A basketball? A basketball.

Mick, who had never been short on words, especially if he was angry, was now rarely heard to speak above a whisper. Even more out of character, he didn't curse at all anymore. This was so unusual for the Crusher that it only confirmed to his acquaintances that he was indeed a few shells short of a full clip. Then there was that smile. Whatever he was doing and wherever he was going, a gentle, happy, and a definitely unthreatening smile graced his street-worn face. It was very troubling.

Some months after his release, Mick entered Mel the Jamaican's clothing store. Mel was behind the short counter that separated him from his customers, and he glanced up when he heard the old brass bell above the door tinkle. Mel choked. He had never liked nor disliked Mick, but he was afraid of him. It was wise to be frightened of someone who was called the Crusher, but not with any measure of affection. As Mick stood in all his arresting presence, Mel slowly inched his left hand toward the side of the counter where he kept his illegal but necessary, sawed-off 12 gauge. It was loaded. Both barrels.

Mick smiled, his face calm and unthreatening. Gentle.

Mel hesitated, frowned, and let his hand drop to his side. Something was different about Mick. He could sense it.

"Whatcha be up to, eh, Mick?" Mel asked, trying his hardest to mask the terror he felt creeping up his spine.

Mick blinked but didn't reply and just flashed that disturbingly unnatural grin.

Mel shuffled his feet and scratched the back of one hand. His skin was crawling with fearful uncertainty. Why was Mick smiling like that? Hadn't he heard that the big thug had become touched in the head—lost his marbles? What did he want?

"You be needing some new clothes then, eh, Mick?"

Mick, his look unchanging, slowly shook his head and let one hand slip into a large pocket of his long, dark coat. Mel's life began to flash before his eyes. He knew his arthritic hand wasn't fast enough to reach the shotgun under the counter, but he wondered why Mick the Crusher was here to kill him. He knew Mick had robbed him more than a couple of times, but he had never gone to the police. He had always viewed the criminal element on the streets around him as an unavoidable and unalterable evil. You just live with it, he had reasoned long ago. To fight against it meant more trouble than it was worth.

Mick's hand lifted from his pocket. Mel quickly closed his eyes and waited, praying softly for his wife. She would miss him. They loved each other. Thirty-two years? No, it was thirty-three. It would be thirty-four in March.

There was a soft thud. Mel jammed his eyes even harder, expecting pain and to feel the strength and life leave what he felt was sure to be his soon-to-be bullet-riddled body. The bell jingled, and Mel opened his eyes. Mick's huge, muscled hand was on the door's edge, while his eyes, serious and steady, were on Mel.

"I'm sorry," said Mick the Crusher, his voice almost too soft and quiet to be heard. But Mel heard.

Mick's face radiated its strange light, his eyes gleaming with something Mel had never thought he would see in them. The Crusher nodded once and pushed his way out into the darkness of the street, letting the door close behind him, the worn brass bell singing its song. Mel swallowed hard, his heart pounding dangerously hard in his heaving chest, and glanced down at the countertop. A roll of cash, bound by a thick rubber band, lay where the Crusher had placed it.

"Mother of God," Mel repeatedly whispered as he counted out five-thousand dollars in hundreds.

Halfway up Fifty-first Street, between Fong's Grocer, with the smoked ducks hanging in the grease-streaked windows, and Bernie's Deli—which really isn't a deli at all but a donut shop—is the seedy alley where Officer Twigge found Mick the Crusher that fateful night, over a year ago. Mick was there now. He had cleaned up the dead-end alley, removing the trash and discarded bits of furniture and rotting things that might have been living things at one time or another. Mick had fashioned a graceful garden along the end wall in the barrenness of the alley that went nowhere. It was a beautiful oasis in a dreary part of the city, filling a third of the alley. At the centre of the garden, shaped somewhat like a walnut, he had built a pond from bricks and concrete and a vinyl lining he had purchased from the building store over on Ninety-second Street. He surrounded it with pots and wooden boxes of ferns, lupines, daisies, marigolds and all sorts of flowers—most with names he didn't remember. He just knew they were beautiful.

Rising out of the middle of the pond, a stylish fake-rock fountain trickled water gently down over its sides, filling the lifeless city air with a beautiful, otherworldly sound and freshness. A dozen goldfish—gold and silver, and some with black spots—lazed in the pond, waiting to be fed. Mick was sitting cross-legged and shoeless in a space he had made amid his garden, carefully pulling little weeds from among the flower pots and, just as carefully, placing them in a self-sealing plastic bag. A tiny yellow canary flitted from one of the pots to the top of the fountain and began to fluff and preen its feathers. Butterflies pranced among the flowers, and bees buzzed and skittered among the petals, seeming unaware of the massive giant tending the lush garden that was out of place in the cavernous brick, grime-streaked walls of the alley.

The giant was smiling and humming and seemed altogether too happy to be someone known as the Crusher.

"Such beauty," Mick said to no one in particular and to the one that would hear.

"Yes," a voice answered, sounding all at once like a thousand golden chimes and the silence of a vast desert, "such beauty."

A spark rose from the colourful flowers of the garden, tiny, brilliant, quick, and paused before Mick. He lifted his eyes to the fiery glow.

"May I?" he asked.

"Yes," the voice sang brightly.

Mick placed the plastic bag of carefully picked weeds between his legs and brushed dirt from his hands, scrubbing at them as if any filth, any stain, was completely intolerable. Then, he held out his right hand, palm up, and the light swiftly settled there. His hand began to glow like a tremendous light had been switched on inside his flesh. The glow expanded, spreading from his fingers to his wrist, disappearing up the arm of his coat to erupt a moment later around his neck, enveloping his entire head. The alley was flooded with light, a brilliant white flame that poured from Mick's head and hands and out from where his socks didn't entirely cover the flesh on his ankles. The whiteness bathed the alley, flooding every crack, chasing every dark shadow away, even where there should have been a shadow. Mick was laughing as tears streamed down his face. His massive frame heaved and jerked with each ripple of joy. Then, slowly, like a dying ember, the light receded until it was just a bright glow again in his palm. A reverent quiet settled over the garden as if the once garbage-strewn alley, which, if it was able, could surely tell stories that would make you lay awake sleepless at night, was, in reality, a majestic cathedral.

Mick wiped the wetness from his face with his other hand. His fingers were trembling. *He* was trembling.

"Why do you not hate me?" he asked, his eyes upon the light floating over his hand. He had asked this before.

"It is not in my nature to hate," the light replied without hesitation.

"But—I killed her."

"Yes."

"Yes. That was the worst moment of my life."

The giant sobbed, and the voice replied.

"Yes. It was."

"I didn't know what I was doing. I thought she was a bug. I always killed bugs. I have always destroyed anything beautiful."

"Yes."

"I'm sorry."

"You are."

"She was so beautiful."

The light sputtered briefly.

"Yes."

"I'm sorry."

Mick wanted to say it a thousand times, a million times, until the pain melted away, until somehow she was no longer dead, crushed by his hatred, until she shone her radiance again until he saw her tiny translucent wings beating in ecstatic rhythm to the striking symphony of her song. No amount of apologies could undo what he had done—undo what he had done all his life—destroy things, crush things. Mick the Crusher.

He wept.

The little light danced, played, and skittered across his hand, across his contorted, pain-filled face, and the voice sang sweetly, harmoniously, like the songs of birds in the spring.

"Alex, Alex, be joyful, Alex. There is beauty. The past is a dream forgotten. What is done is over; what is now is present."

As has happened many times before, Alex—Mick— felt his heart lift with the forgiveness he did not deserve.

There was a sound behind them, someone clearing their throat. Mick turned his head and nodded. The light (he didn't know what else to call it, and the concept of a name for itself had made no sense to it) flew from his hand and began to sweep in tight, excited circles around the visitor.

"Hello," officer Milton Twigge said, removing his police hat as he laughed, letting the spark settle on his hand. "Am I interrupting anything?"

Mick rose slowly to his feet.

"No, Milton, please join us."

"Yes," sang the light, its song vibrating with approval along the rigid walls of the alley.

Officer Twigge and Mick the Crusher embraced each other—David and Goliath—and the light darted in between their arms and touched them, and the two men exploded with brilliance as if they were standing in the blaze of midday sunlight. The spark sang and danced and played songs upon the air, and Milton and Mick stepped back to watch, laughing, giddy, like little children. If seeing Mick the Crusher smile with hidden joy was unnerving, this was even more so. The giant fist of the Crusher had now become the hand of friendship to the one who had arrested him more times than either felt necessary to recall.

"I heard what you did today—for Mel," Milton said after a moment, speaking as if he were standing in a hallowed place.

"Yes." Mick nodded, holding his hand out to the dancing light. It twirled between his outstretched fingers.

"Will you invite him here?" Twigge touched the arm of his friend, his old adversary. "Like you did, me?"

"If he'd like that."

Milton nodded and sighed. "I'm glad. It's beautiful here, in this alley."

"Yes," the voice trilled with effervescent excitement, "beauty."

Mick nodded, agreeing.

"Beauty."

Note: *Touched - The idea for this story came to me after a visit to Oxford, England, where I saw gardens wedged into any available space. No matter how small, they added a slice of beauty amid red brick and ancient history.*

4. I'VE CROSSED OVER

I'VE CROSSED OVER.

I never saw it coming. I was blindsided, like turning a corner and walking head-on into a closed door. That was how I felt as I stood at the Save On Foods "Eleven Items or Less" checkout counter. I had three items: a tube of Arm and Hammer Ultimate Whitening toothpaste, a tin of No Name low sodium cashews, and a three-pack of Dentyne Cinnamon-Fresh chewing gum.

I arrived at the store moments before closing, specifically to buy the toothpaste, but, well, those items they stock at the checkout always bewitch me.

No one else was in line at the till, so the cashier and I chatted it up a bit. Yes, the evenings were getting cooler, but the stars were nice to see again; and yes, toothpaste is expensive, but well, not as expensive as a visit to the dentist. You know, simple idle conversation between two people who weren't strangers but perhaps could be considered acquaintances by way of association. I had seen her and one or two of her children on a soccer field over the years, and, of course, she worked at the grocery store nearest my home.

"Don't you have a son in soccer?" she casually asked while scanning the toothpaste.

"Yes," I answered, then corrected myself, "Did, actually. He just turned twenty and hung the cleats up a while ago."

She nodded and smiled.

"Mine just went off to university."

"Oh? Where?"

"Edinburgh, Scotland."

"Mine leaves for community college after Christmas," I countered.

She nodded, her till beeping as she scanned the cashews, and then asked, "How many children do you have?"

"Two."

She scanned the Dentyne.

"I have three."

"Oh," I said, wondering if she felt giving birth to more children than I qualified her for some kind of crown of maternal achievement. So, foolishly, I tried to one-up her. "My youngest just turned twenty."

"Ah, yes, you mentioned that."

"Oh, right."

I chuckled, feeling the sting of embarrassment.

"Well, you're in that place," she said, her expression suddenly switching to one of sympathy.

I frowned.

"What place?"

"You know, *the* place."

"I don't understand."

"No more children."

She did a half laugh and raised her eyebrows as if she had just stated the blatantly obvious.

Suddenly, I felt the smile freeze on my face. That's when I walked full-on into that proverbial shut door. The very definition by which I had qualified a good part of my reason for existing over the last twenty or so years was immediately and rudely wrenched from my grasp and forever altered. Without parade or fanfare, I was no longer a mother *with* children. I had become *the* mother of *adult* children. At that very moment, I felt myself cross over. It was almost spiritual, a definable shift in my reality, like the apprehension accompanying that first menstrual period that launched me into womanhood or the final, painful contraction that threw me into motherhood. I was about to become something I had not been.

"Nineteen, thirty-six."

I was old.

"Ma'am?"

I *am* old.

"That'll be nineteen, thirty-six, please."

I focused on her face. There was a hint of playfulness in her eyes. She *knew* what I was feeling.

"How old is your youngest?" I abruptly asked, hoping to return the favour of this uncomfortable revelation.

Her smile slowly grew.

"Twenty-one."

"Oh," I muttered as I handed her two tens. She had already gone where I was now standing.

"It hurts, doesn't it?" she said, taking the bills as our fingers briefly touched.

"Hurts?"

"No more children. It changes who you are." The till popped open, and she began fishing coins out as she continued, "They grow up. Move out. Get on with their adult lives. Now, all the mismatched socks belong to either you or your husband. You can no longer blame your children for anything that gets broken or goes missing, or for that glob of peanut butter and jelly on the kitchen floor," she paused to draw in a breath, "or a thousand other little things that happened every day of every week of every month, but don't anymore."

She dropped coins into my hand, counting out the twenty with a deliberate finality. I slowly closed my fingers tightly around their cold hardness.

"And," she said, placing her hand gently over mine, "the silence. The house is so quiet."

"Oh?"

"Are your parents alive?"

"Yes."

"Do they live here?"

"No. Out east."

"Do you visit them often?"

"As often as I can. I don't—"

"Do you have any brothers and sisters?"

"Yes. Well, two brothers, but—"

"After you and your brothers left home, did you notice that whenever you returned to visit and you were watching television with your parents, it seemed as if they had the volume set way too loud?"

"I guess."

I nodded hesitantly, wondering where she was going with this even odder turn in our conversation.

"You see, it's not only that they are aging and losing their hearing, but also because the non-stop noise and activity that accompanies raising children is no longer present. Those endless morning-until-night marathons of running to this child's class play and that child's after-school event, and this one's weekend soccer tournament, and all those countless trips to the mall," she paused, raising a hand and groping the air like a Shakespearean actor, "have been replaced with the deafening sound of silence."

Her hand collapsed into a tight fist, "And you are faced with the crushing reality of 'What do you do now with all this time?'"

She suddenly blushed as if aware of her somewhat dramatic oratory. She quickly bagged my three items and handed them to me along with my receipt. Feeling disoriented and adrift in unfamiliar waters, I turned to leave. I had just come for toothpaste. I hadn't expected to have a life-altering encounter. It made me angry, and I wanted to scream. I wanted to run home, paint the kitchen counter with peanut butter and strawberry jam, and leave sticky fingerprints on the hallway walls. In the upstairs closet was a box of old toys—G.I. Joes, Transformers, and Lego—that I could scatter across the living room floor. I hadn't stepped on a toy in years. It wasn't fair.

Afraid that she might sense the anger rippling beneath my tight smile, I mumbled my thanks and began to walk away but then stopped. She, this middle-aged cashier, had thrown me a lifeline. This woman was obviously familiar with that place where I had just now belly-flopped.

I turned back to her.

"So, um—"

"What do you do now?" she finished, her expression sympathetic and all-knowing.

I nodded slowly, my heart an empty but anxious vessel of expectation.

She reached across the space between us and patted my arm.

"Go home, honey, and turn up the television."

Note: *I've Crossed Over - This story is mostly true. The epiphany moment happened for me in a gas station convenience store, where the clerk, whose son had played soccer with one of mine, made me realize that the end of the child-rearing part of my identity had somehow quietly slipped away.*

5. A CONVERSATION

AS USUAL, SALLY WAS LATE. It irritated Tate that he often sat alone, waiting for her, and feeling stupid every time the waitress came over to refill his coffee cup. And the restaurant's wooden chairs were hard and uncomfortable. He had often wondered if not being on time was deliberate, though he had never voiced this accusation. Not that it mattered anymore; today, he was breaking up with her.

Tate had met Sally for breakfast every day of the week for the last year, except on Sundays. On Sundays, she took the transit to a little church up on Maple Street. He didn't go with her. Churches made Tate uncomfortable. The daily rendezvous seemed a trifle formal now, considering their first encounter had been quite casual. Still, he felt the rapport between them had developed into something requiring further commitment

—from her at least. There should have been greater respect, he felt, for the effort he had invested into the relationship.

Sally casually approached the table and slid gracefully into one of its four plastic chairs. It was the same chair she always sat in. Tate believed it was some inexplicably strange personal obsession for her to choose that particular table and chair day after day. Indeed, the logic of her action eluded him. Furthermore, it bugged him because it meant he had to sit facing the door, where the sea of customers who frequented the place was constantly distracting him.

"Hello," he said, smiling and appearing sincerely pleased to see her despite the tardy arrival. He wasn't sure how she would respond to the breakup. He needed to be as charming as possible.

She said nothing in reply, dropping her heavy black purse to the floor beside her and snagging one of the menus that sat propped between a bottle of ketchup and hot sauce. He sighed, bit his lower lip, and flipped open a menu.

Ham and eggs with a side order of hash browns, pepper, and no salt. Eggs, sunny side up. Earl Grey tea with a bit of milk, but no sugar, and orange juice, but no pulp. That's what she would order. She always did, except for that one time when she'd had that foul, lingering head cold and ordered a bowl of Red River cereal and black coffee.

He observed her intently, over the top of the menu. She was attired in her black pinstripe executive suit with that silk, frilled shirt that was as white as snow. The neckline was low enough to reveal a tantalizing slip of black lace bra. He liked that bra. It was chic and suggested an almost Eurocentric sophistication. He would miss that quality of who she was, he realized. Her long, slender legs, wrapped in silky black stockings, disappeared into narrow, glossy, black Versace pumps. She also owned a green and a red pair of the fashionably expensive shoes. Her shoulder-length hair appeared, as always, as if she had just left Monique's over on Fifth. She walked there from where she worked in an uptown real estate office every third Friday at noon, during her lunch break. Like everything else about Sally, her makeup was flawless. Every morning she laboured at great length to prepare that delicate, heart-shaped face to meet the day. He loved watching her pluck eyebrows, shape eyelashes, and cleanse her soft, creamy skin. She would paint her full lips a deep red, the colour of sweet dark cherries, and line her eyes, so they were dark, radiant, and inviting. It was akin to watching a master artisan at work, he felt, and he would miss all this, too.

Oh, how he adored her, loved the smell of her hair and the lovely sound of her voice. Tate could think of nothing he didn't find irresistible about her. Even her name, Sally Georgina Kramstead, was like a symphony that played over and over in his mind, enthralling his heart, enlivening his long, dreary days. He dreamed of her every moment, and his heart ached for the love they shared to become unbridled in its passion, but it was too late. As much as he smouldered with love for her, he wasn't convinced she felt the same toward him.

The waitress approached the table, and he nodded to Sally. Ladies first. Tate always insisted she ordered first, no matter how long the waitress stood there waiting for him if she wasn't quite ready.

Briskly, as always, she rattled off her breakfast order. It was rote for her. The waitress cleared her throat and arced her eyebrows toward him, and today Tate did something he's never done before—he ordered a three-cheese breakfast burrito and a tall glass of chocolate milk.

This was a new day in Tate's life. He was going to close the book on this tragic love story, and his resolution required a dramatic change, something radical. The first of many changes, he vowed.

"Did you sleep well?" he asks curtly as the waitress walks away with the orders.

She looks up, smiles tightly and turns her face away. Why does she do that, he asks himself. I asked her a question. Am I not worthy of an answer? This was the real reason he was breaking up with her. He had to do all the talking and work to maintain the relationship. He always bared his soul to her and expressed his eternal love and affection.

On the other hand, she never told him exactly how she felt. Oh, she had nodded, smiled beautifully (as she always did), shrugged, and mumbled things, but that was all she seemed to care to contribute. How could a person, so obviously lovely, so demonstrably the image of perfection, seem so ugly inside? It was painful, excruciatingly, and the relationship lacked any tangible reward, and Tate had had enough.

"We need to have a conversation, Sally."

Her eyes met his, they were expressionless, and then she reached down, pulling a magazine from her purse. Esquire. She loved Esquire. He hated that magazine.

"Listen," he said, his fingers drumming in annoyance on the scarred surface of the table. "We need to talk."

Sally placed the magazine in the centre of the table and began flipping through the pages, from back to front. He hated that, too. It was unbearably annoying, like fingernails on a chalkboard to him. He had once asked her why she did that, read the magazine backwards. As usual, she hadn't bothered with a reply; she just smiled pleasantly—like what he thought didn't hold an ounce of weight in her life—and kept turning the pages, from back to front.

"Fine," he spat, hoping his anger would shock her. It didn't seem to matter, however. She continued to graze through the glossy pages of the magazine.

"Whatever," he mumbled.

The waitress interrupted his brooding, arriving with Sally's food. She thanked the waitress. It was the first thing she had said since arriving, and it wasn't even addressed toward him. Tate bit his lip hard. Without a doubt, it was over now.

"Go ahead, eat. I'll talk then."

She lifted a forkful of eggs to her lips, shrugged, and turned a page.

Tate talked. His courage was armed, his thoughts clear and ordered, and his words as precise as he could muster. He told her how he felt, how he despised being ignored and treated as if his needs and wants were irrelevant to her. It infuriated him, made him feel useless and impotent, and it caused him to wonder if the bond between them was worth the effort he had poured into it.

"Twelve months," he bristled. "Twelve months, and this is all we have?"

Breakfast, sometimes lunch, or the occasional movie night where they didn't even sit together. What kind of date was that? Was she embarrassed, ashamed to be seen in public with him? Did she think he was not her social or intellectual equal? Was she seeing someone else? There was someone else, wasn't there? Where did that red rose he had found last Monday in that delicate pink vase on the kitchen table come from? He hadn't given it to her. The dozen roses he had given her, one for each month of their relationship, had ended up in the trash bin. Why? And whose black socks were in the laundry last week? They belonged to another man, didn't they? And, what about that letter in the mailbox? It was a card, a sappy, sweet Hallmark card. It smelled of cologne and was signed, "Phil." Phil who?

Once in a while, Sally nodded, but her expression remained indifferent. She looked out the window, forked hash browns into her pretty, perfect mouth, sipped her tea, and flipped pages of her magazine. She took a moment to slice her thick piece of ham into six parts (like she always did), but not once did she offer him the respect of her attention or comment on his raw and heartfelt rant. In fact, she had the nerve to look up once and smile at Tate as he poured his frustrations out like spilled coffee on the table. That only antagonized him further, and his voice escalated, and his fingers began to pound the table like a jackhammer. When the waitress finally brought his burrito and chocolate milk, she placed it before him and quickly retreated.

Tate wanted to lash out and talk some sense into Sally to make her understand. He was a good man, a faithful friend and an attentive lover. Hadn't he met with her every morning for the last year and tolerated her supercilious, egotistical behaviour? Didn't he deserve better? Could she find anyone more devoted than he?

Tate didn't see the police officer standing next to the table until the man tapped him on the shoulder.

"Excuse me, sir," the officer said, one hand resting confidently on his holstered weapon, the other holding a threatening-looking black baton.

"I'm going to have to ask you to quiet down and finish your meal."

Tate glared incredulously at the officer—at the intrusion. It had taken long, agonizing weeks to finally gather enough courage to articulate these intimate and revealing thoughts to Sally, and nothing was going to interfere, especially not now.

"Hey, can't you see I am having a conversation here?" He blurted, his voice crackling with an emotion he struggled to contain.

The police officer's eyes travelled around the table.

"A conversation, sir? With whom?"

Tate sputtered, groaned in the deepest, most profound sense of exasperation he had ever felt, and shoved the chair back harshly as he rose to his feet.

"Are you daft? I'm having a conversation with my girlfriend, of course."

The officer smiled—but it wasn't a pleasant expression—as he surveyed the empty wooden chairs around the table.

"Sir, I'm going to ask you to leave the restaurant with me."

Something inside Tate snapped. He was having the most important conversation of his life, he was breaking up with Sally, and this uninvited person, this callous, thoughtless, gun-toting Neanderthal, was robbing him— no— he was stripping him of this glorious, triumphant moment.

He was breaking up with Sally!

As he drove his tightly balled fist into the officer's face, Tate wondered if the man's name might be Phil.

Sally looked up from her Esquire magazine and glanced out the restaurant window. A metallic reflection caught her attention. Across the narrow pedestrian street, in a diner she had only eaten in once before, about a year ago, a man was lying face down on a table. She could just see his head and shoulders through the window, and, for a moment, their eyes met. A daunting police officer was struggling to handcuff the man.

When the officer pulled him upright, Sally caught her breath. It was that guy who had sat at the same table, day after day. She had often seen him watching her while she ate. He talked to himself. Sally suddenly felt a chill; she had never really liked the way he would just stare at her.

Note: *A Conversation - Many people struggle with mental health. It's a reality of the world we live in. Unfortunately, it's often seen as a moral failure rather than an actual, treatable illness. This story is loosely based on someone I knew who went untreated for most of his life.*

6. iDEAD

HAL CALLAHAN AWOKE and immediately wished he hadn't. The pain slowly and rhythmically radiated out from his left side, from around his barely active and only remaining kidney. Callahan opened his eyes slowly, fighting the ever-present sensation of nausea. The room was dark. He turned his head, even though it hurt to do so, just enough so he could see the oversized, blue digital numbers on the clock on his night table. 2:36. He groaned, then groaned again. Even the effort it took to growl his discomfort from behind his compressed lips was painful. He had only been asleep for over half an hour since the last time he was slammed awake by the ravaging demon of pain. It was going to be another long night.

"Penny?"

His nurse answered immediately, her voice a bodiless comfort in the darkness, "Yes, Mr. Callahan."

"Hal. Please call me Hal."

"Yes, Hal."

"More drip, please."

"I am sorry, Hal, I am unable to complete your request."

"I'm hurting here."

"I am sorry, Hal. You will exceed the recommended dosage for this time cycle."

"I'm in pain," he pleaded.

"Yes, your serotonin levels are elevated, your heart rate is—"

"Can you—?"

"I am sorry, Hal."

"Anything? Something?"

"I can offer fifty milligrams of class two non-narcotic pain inhibitor. This may assist you in returning to a reasonable level of comfort for a few moments."

Callahan grunted carefully.

"Very well. You're a tough one, aren't you?"

"Your health is my priority, Mr. Callahan."

"Right, and call me Hal."

"Yes, Hal. Please accept my apology."

A feeling of calming warmth began to flow outward from his left forearm where the IV was connected, promising a reprise from the agony.

"Penny?"

"Yes, Mr. Callahan?"

"Hal."

"Yes, Hal?"

"Could you bring up the lights?"

"Do you wish to rise? I will need assistance."

"No, I just want to have a look at Emma."

"How many lumens?"

"Six or so?"

The light strip around the edge of the ceiling suddenly glowed like the light from a handful of candles, and Hal turned his head again towards the nightstand.

"Thank you, Penny."

"You are quite welcome, Hal."

Emma smiled at him from the photo next to the clock. She seemed so young, so vivacious. She was. The image was taken almost forty years ago, three decades before cancer robbed his wife of her looks and life. It would soon take his.

"Penny?"

"Yes, Hal?"

"Can I talk to you?"

"Of course, Hal. Do you wish to discuss today's weather or the latest newscast?"

"Is it raining? I like the rain."

"No, I am sorry, it is not raining. The temperature is 32 Celsius, with winds of 2.5 kilometres from the Southeast. The dew point is—"

"Could we talk about Emma?"

"Of course, Hal. What era of her life do you wish to discuss?"

"I just wanted to talk."

"Of course, Hal."

"She was beautiful."

"Yes, I have seen her file. She was quite lovely."

"We farmed in Alberta."

"Yes, south of Vulcan."

"We milked a couple of hundred head of Guernsey."

"Yes."

"Emma was right there with me. Slingin' hay and slopping hogs with the best of the hired hands."

"You raised pigs?"

"Yeah, for slaughter. I miss bacon. I can still smell it sometimes, even in here."

Callahan let his eyes slip away from the photograph. It hurt to keep his head turned to the side for that long anyway.

"We had a dog. Several over the years."

"Yes. Max. Pug. Dolly."

"Brutus," he interrupted her, recounting the names of the pet dogs he had obviously told her about before. Though, he couldn't quite remember when he had done so.

"Yes. Brutus. A lab collie cross."

"Yeah. Loved that dog. Used to chase the chickens, though."

Penny laughed. Callahan shifted slightly. He wished he could feel his legs, even if for one more time. He had enjoyed their stoic strength, but it seemed so long ago.

"Are you comfortable, Hal?" His nurse asked.

Callahan sighed.

"Just feeling my age."

"You are one-hundred and twenty-nine, Hal."

He guffawed and immediately wished he hadn't. "Ouch. Thanks for reminding me."

"You are quite welcome."

"I was being facetious."

Penny laughed.

"I am aware of your humour.

"I *am* old."

"Yes, but you have lived a meaningful and productive life."

Callahan nodded slightly.

"I suppose."

"You and Emma raised two sons."

"Uh-huh."

Barton, the eldest, and Montgomery, but he had only seen Barton and his wife and their three daughters, his only grandchildren, once since entering the home over three years ago. Monty, who never seemed to find time for a relationship with anyone, had sent him a Christmas card the year before, but his lanky son had not visited. Not even once.

The home provided his every need, Monty had simply

said in an email. What was there for him to do except sit and watch his father die, he wouldn't have it. Emma had lived and then died in this same institution. Callahan felt a twinge of guilt upon realizing that he, too had eventually come to visit her only every other month. He hadn't needed to, he had reasoned many times. The institution took excellent care of her, as they had taken very good care of him. He would die without any need, except maybe the touch of another human being.

Soon, he allowed himself to romanticize, he would be with his wife. The colon cancer had stricken his body, stripping his strength, leaving him gaunt and a shadow of the brawny hard-working man he'd once been. However, it was his heart that would eventually kill him. Too many miles on the old ticker, the doctors had informed him, and just too old for another transplant, from a donor, or genetically engineered, or otherwise. Penny had already resuscitated him four times over the last five days, clawing him back from the abyss. His nurse was an excellent and highly skilled caregiver, Callahan knew, but he was tired of living, and he had asked that he not be revived should his heart fail again. It was time to be with Emma.

"Do you wish to continue this conversation, Hal?"

"No, that's all right. Thank you, Penny."

"You are quite welcome, Mr. Callahan."

"Hal."

"Hal. Do you wish the lighting returned to normal for this cycle?"

"That'd be fine."

The room immediately grew dark, and all that Callahan could hear was the soft hum of the life support machines that flanked his bed and the rasp of his breathing. He felt a sudden wave of sorrow; he could no longer recall the sound of Emma's breathing next to him. He missed her touch. He longed to—

"Mr. Callahan?"

"Hal."

"Hal."

"Yes, Penny?"

"Your breathing is laboured, and your pulse has risen fourteen percent in the last two point seven minutes. You are experiencing significant discomfort."

He was. His chest hurt like his rib cage was trapped in the jaws of a crushing vise.

"I am having a hard time breathing."

The room light brightened enough for Callahan to see.

"Your heart is failing," his nurse said.

"Am I going to die?"

"That is a likely prognosis, Hal."

"Do … NOT …" he gasped. "resuscitate me."

"The DNR request has been noted on your chart."

The alarm began to sound on his heart monitor. It was loud. Annoying.

"Turn—that off."

The beeping stopped.

"Penny."

"Yes, Hal."

"Could you hold my hand?"

"I am unable to do so, Hal."

"I know."

It hurt. Hurt like nothing he'd ever felt. It was even worse than the cancer. He wanted it to end.

"Penny?"

"Yes."

"Thank you."

"You are quite welcome, Mr. Callahan."

"Hal."

It was the last word Callahan spoke.

"Yes. Hal."

Callahan did not hear the reply.

Penny spoke quietly.

"Pulse: none. Respiration: none. Brain function: insignificant."

The room flooded with brilliant light as the machine noise faded.

"Patient 412956-078ND has ceased to exist. Request notification of relatives and removal of remains."

A voice, as efficient and monotone as Penny's, replied from a speaker somewhere in the ceiling above the lifeless body of Hal Callahan.

"Patient 412956-078ND's cease of life functions are noted. Time of death noted as 2:59 A.M. Immediate relatives contacted and notified. Do you confirm,

PNE511C?"

"Confirmed."

"You may log off for internal diagnostics, PNE511C. You will be assigned to patient 483501-341ND, room 4033, level 45, section C, at 1100 hours. Confirm."

"Confirm."

PNE511C bio-scanned the still form of Henry Montgomery Callahan one more time, adding the biometrics to his medical database. The immediate relatives would require the information for insurance purposes.

"Goodbye, Mr. Callahan," PNE511C said.

Personal Nursing Entity 511C logged off.

Note: iDead, as far as I know, is a term that I have coined to describe the possible future of long-term medical care. Death and dying are an inconvenience to our lives, and modern humans, at least in the West, have gone to great lengths to avoid this inevitable part of our journey. One has to only look at the sterile long-term care facilities we hustle our elderly off to.

7. A PRAIRIE YARN

ALBERT PLIMPTON WIPED THE SHEEN of sweat from his forehead with the monogrammed handkerchief his wife had given him for their twentieth wedding anniversary. Long ago, the material had been a brilliant white, but now the cotton was thin and a dirty shade of grey. Shirley had meticulously cross-stitched a simple A. P. in the bottom right corner. God knew she wasn't much of a seamstress, but she had tried, and he loved her for that. Now, almost a dozen years later, the letters were a mere hint of their former reddish hue, and the P was missing its leg, making it look like an odd-shaped O. He chuckled, playing with the fleeting moment of happiness the memory brought before carefully folding the well-used gift and stuffing it in a back pocket of his overalls.

Straining to reach behind him, he picked up the heavy pipe wrench he had placed on the mechanical floor's cold concrete. The faucet he was focused on was difficult to reach and had not seen the light of day for years, not for decades perhaps. Albert pulled a ball-peen hammer from his utility belt with his other hand and tapped lightly on the sides of the rust-encrusted faucet. Flecks of rotted metal dropped to the floor. Satisfied, he dropped the hammer and maneuvered his ample bulk to get both hands on the wrench. He pushed, pulled, jerked and tried to angle as much leverage as his arms could muster until he felt a slight movement. Grinning with a sense of impending victory, Albert pushed even harder. With a terrible grinding sound, the valve suddenly snapped and pulled away from the old brick wall it was anchored to. Water geysered out from the broken pipe, slamming into Albert's face and chest. Choking and cursing, he scrambled back, banging his head on the underside of the cluttered worktable where he had jimmied his upper body to reach the faucet. He loudly chastised himself.

You should have shut the main off, Al, he thought angrily.

The shut-off was an arms-length away, and it took only a few quick turns of the valve to stifle the icy water flow.

Albert was soaked. He didn't particularly enjoy the water, other than in a glass with lots of ice, or hot, in a bathtub, but he was a seasoned plumber, and that meant he would, more often than not, lose the battle with his elemental nemesis. That hadn't mattered much when he was younger, but now that he was edging closer to seventy, Albert had less patience for the discomforts of his long career. He grunted and struggled to his feet, wishing he hadn't let himself get out of shape as much as he had. He could shed fifty pounds, he thought, at least that much, anyway. If Shirley could see him now, he mused, she'd have him on a diet so fast his head would've spun clean off his fat shoulders. He fumbled around for his tools. These he slid into his belt, using a rag to wipe them dry before doing so.

"Weeeell," he said to the empty room as he glanced at his water-splattered watch. 8:15. "I think I hav'ta call it a day."

That was when the pain lanced Albert like a knife. It began in the pinky finger of his left hand and shot up to his shoulder as if someone had shoved a crimson-hot poker clear through his arm. He screamed as the agony slammed into his chest, causing his legs to buckle beneath him. He fell to his knees hard and then tumbled over onto his side, his head clipping the metal leg of the worktable. Specks, flitting about like angry bees, filled his vision as his lungs struggled to draw air. He felt like a truckload of timber had suddenly crashed onto his chest.

Albert was dying, and he knew it.

"Oh, God," he gasped, "not now... not now...."

Gibraltar. He and Shirley were going to Gibraltar in March. Gibraltar. The sea. Not now. He had promised to spread her ashes on the shores of the Mediterranean. Not now. No—

"Albert?"

His head hurt.

"Albert? Wake up, honey."

Albert became aware of the pink glow of light from behind his eyelids. It must be morning, except—there were no windows in the apartment building's utility room. The pain. His chest. Was he in the hospital? He opened his eyes and searched for the face of the voice that had spoken to him.

"Hello, Sweetie."

What? He knew that face—from twenty years ago. Shirley. His wife. Shirley before… Wait, this wasn't possible. He was hallucinating. He had banged his head on the worktable.

I must have a concussion.

Albert sat up quickly, and his head throbbed as if a jackhammer was pounding a hole behind his left ear.

"Ouch," he griped, reaching a hand up to rub the spot.

"Whoa there, Big Boy," his wife said, her dazzling, expansive smile consuming her face, "You had yourself quite a fall."

"What?" he managed to ask.

"I told you not to go up on the roof without Benny's help."

"What?" He asked again, staring at her but not daring to believe what he saw. His wife was dead—had been for more than a dozen years. Breast cancer. They discovered the lumps too late, and she had died a tragic and painful death.

Shirley turned her head away, her dark curls

bouncing lightly, and spoke to someone just out of Albert's sight, "Hey Doc, is my husband gonna live or do I get to collect on the insurance?"

Albert turned to see to whom his wife was talking. Doctor Alex Murphy was standing beside another bed and taking the temperature of a young boy. Didn't old Doc Murphy die last year? Albert recognized the kid. Stanley Kowalski. Hadn't the Kowalski kid been killed in a rollover on Highway 565?

What the hell is going on?

Doc Murphy smiled at Albert and winked. "He's still got a few years in 'im, Shirley."

Albert's mouth was dry like a mouthful of straw, but he pried his lips apart and grabbed Shirley's hand. "Am I dead?"

Her large dark eyes, so painfully familiar, frowned at him, and she looked at the doctor again, "Doc?"

"Take him home, Shirley. Put 'im to bed. Doctor's orders." And he laughed, the sound of his voice like a ghost from the past.

But Albert wouldn't let go of her hand or the question.

"Am I dead?"

Shirley shook her head, frowning as if he'd just asked the stupidest question in the entire universe. Then she hugged him, pulling him tight, one gentle hand cupped to the back of his head. "Of course not, you big lug."

She smelled so good, so familiar, and so desirable that he began to sob. His heart was breaking. His wife was dead. He reached his arms around her lithe frame and held onto her as if it were their last moment on Earth. There had been that terrible day when it had been their last.

"Oh, my, my little plumber. What's come over you?" he heard her ask.

"You're dead," he choked.

She pulled back and squashed his face between her small but firm hands, smudging his tears with her thumbs.

"Right, Sweetie. You are not getting that insurance money this easily."

Then she slid her hands down to his shoulders and helped him up. Albert let her. He suddenly felt foolish. She was obviously alive, or this was one hell of a great dream. More of a flashback, really, he thought. He did fall off the roof once while cleaning the chimney, but that was a couple of decades ago.

"See ya, Doc," his wife said as they headed for the ward door. "Thanks a bunch."

"Any time, Shirley. Take care of that man of yours." Doc Murphy answered, winking at Albert. "Mind your wife now, Albert. Get some rest."

Albert nodded and smiled. Why was he dreaming about this event? It seemed so real. It felt like he was really back there, like he was twenty years younger, still had a full head of hair, and Benny hadn't gone to college yet. Back when Shirley was still healthy, young and sexy. He patted her behind.

She reacted immediately, grabbing his hand and holding it tight in hers, "Hey, Tiger." Her smouldering dark eyes met his. "I see your libido wasn't injured in the fall."

She winked at him. God, it was so real.

They made love that night. It was heated, passionate lovemaking, filled with whispered sweet things, ending with the two of them falling asleep, Albert holding desperately onto her. He had missed her and felt so lost without her, but he had moved on, buried the grief in his work. He had to, or the unbearable pain of losing his son would have killed him.

When he awoke early the following day, she was still there, lying naked beside him, in their bed, in their house, still twenty years ago. What kind of dream was this? Was he in a coma from what he supposed was a heart attack? Did people relive their lives while in a coma, he wondered as he slowly slid out of bed and padded softly to Benny's room. The door was slightly ajar. He eased it open so he could see his son, asleep, one leg poking out from the comforter his mother had made for him. It was so good to see him, and he felt the tears he had shed alone for their son begin to rise again. He blinked and looked away. He didn't want to disturb his son—tall, dark-haired, athletic Benny.

The kid was only seventeen, then—but, God, he was so bright and eager to finish his last year of high school. He had his sights set on a technical school out east. He would go, and he would graduate, and then his mother would die, and he and Albert would gradually and painfully cease talking to each other. He couldn't explain why; it just happened, like Shirley's death. Then, lost like his father, Benny, would join the Armed Forces. He needed to do something worthwhile, he had said. Less than a year later, he would step on a roadside IED, and Albert would be alone.

He padded softly downstairs to the living room and slid into his leather lounger, which didn't look as good as it did in this dream, he mused. He snagged the remote from the coffee table and flipped the power on the television, and switched it to one of the news channels. Grain reports. Metals down. Weather. Sunny most of the day, with some wind with a chance of showers in the evening. The farmers would like that. *Had* enjoyed that, he corrected himself. Mulroney was off to Washington to chat with Reagan over the North American Free Trade Agreement. He laughed softly at that. Twenty years later, NAFTA was still a mixed blessing for most and a downright curse for others. Some local news: a minor truck fire over at the mill; a two-car collision, no one injured; some kids painted a cow pink (he marvelled that he remembered that); and the missing three-year-old child, Alice Featherington, had not been found yet.

Albert hunched forward. He knew where Alice Featherington was. She had wandered off from her family's farmhouse and had fallen into a steep-walled ravine. It was almost impossible to see her, even from the bottom of the prairie scar, or to hear her cries for help unless you knew where to look. Her father would find her decomposed body the following spring.

Wasn't that ravine a couple of miles from his own home? It was. He had gone there shortly after they'd found the little girl's body, just to look and see where she had died. It was a heartbreaking day for the community.

Albert stood up, smiling. Now, this was a dream he liked. He could change the past, alter the future, and control destiny. For a moment, he wondered if he could fly. He liked dreams where he flew. First things first, he reasoned, and he slipped back into the bedroom to dress.

He stubbed his foot against the bed and woke Shirley with his yelp. She smiled broadly, running a hand through her tussled hair.

"Hey, tiger. I'm still swooning from last night. What got into you?"

He grinned boyishly and bent over her and kissed her long and passionately.

"Where you off to?" she moaned as he pulled away.

Should he tell her? What the hell, why not? It was only a dream, after all.

"I know where that Featherington child is."

Shirley sat up, pulling the quilt around her.

"What? They found her?"

He grinned.

"No, not yet."

"But, you said—"

"I know where she is. I'm heading out there right now to get her."

Shirley swung her legs out and stood, pulling the quilt with her, holding it tighter around her.

"I don't get it. You know where Mabel's girl is?"

He nodded, cinching up his belt. He couldn't believe what great shape he had been in back then. When he woke up from this coma, he promised himself he would take better care of his body.

"Al, you're not making sense. How is it you know where she is?"

He drew her close, kissing her forehead.

"Because this is my dream. This happened twenty years ago, and I know where they will find her months from now."

She frowned like she had yesterday when he had asked her if he was dead.

"Your dream?"

"Yes. Alice Feathering died from exposure. It was a terrible thing. This is my dream, and I can change that, maybe even change what happened to you."

He turned to leave, but Shirley grabbed his arm. "What do you mean, 'change what happened to me?'"

It's a dream, he told himself. He could do whatever he wanted and change anything, anything at all.

"Come with me."

The frown did not leave her face.

"To find Alice?"

"To find Alice."

"You're serious?"

He shrugged.

"What the hell? It's my dream."

Shirley said very little as she dressed, much to Albert's disappointment. He had wondered if he could control what she would say or do, but it hadn't worked, no matter how hard he focused his thoughts on her. He began to think that maybe this was one of those dreams that carried you along for the ride. It took her only a few moments to dress, brush her hair into something manageable, and grab a couple of apples and travel mugs of instant coffee made from hot tap water. Minutes later, they were in the Chevy, charting a course through the awakening streets, heading for the edge of town and the intersection of RR 33 and Highway 561. The ravine was not far from where the road formed a junction with the rural route, about a kilometre past the intersection, Albert turned off onto the gravel road that led out to the Featherington's farm. A moment later, he turned onto an even rougher and dustier track that quickly ended at the crack in the face of the Alberta prairie.

Shirley launched herself from the vehicle and called Alice's name, but they heard no reply. Albert knew they wouldn't. Volunteer searchers and even dogs had gone over this area, but the missing child hadn't been found, not until long after she had died.

Albert led his wife down an old cow path that snaked into the ravine. The child's father, he remembered, had found her body at the far end, trapped between two boulders. A heavy overhang of sod had fallen on top of her, effectively hiding her from searching eyes until the spring thaw months later. Her decomposing body had slumped sideways into view.

"This way," he directed, taking Shirley's hand.

"You're sure?" she asked.

"I came here after they found her. I was curious."

"After? You mean, in your dream?"

He laughed as he lifted her into the rocky bottom of the old riverbed.

"This is my dream, and you are beautiful."

Shirley smiled, returning his youthful kiss, but he could tell she was worried about him. She probably suspected he was still delusional after he fell from the roof, and she was playing along. Albert didn't care, he was enjoying himself. It was fascinating to manipulate his dreams like this, especially if it meant he could change the outcome of a tragic event, even if only in the dream.

As they neared the place where Albert knew Alice had been found, he began to call out the girl's name. Shirley heard the pitiful cries first.

"Oh, my God," his wife gasped as he began to pull the dirt and rocks away from where the little girl had been trapped.

Alice was there, dirty, soiled, face streaked with muddy tears, but alive. Feeling immense personal satisfaction, Albert lifted the edge of the large clump of sod that had trapped her, and Shirley pulled the girl free.

"I can't believe this, Albert," his wife cried, trying to remain calm for the child's sake. "How could you have known she was here?"

Albert brushed debris from the girl's dress and matted hair and beamed, "This is my dream."

"Enough already about that, Albert. How did you know?"

How did he know? This *was* his dream. He *would* know, wouldn't he?

Albert drove in troubled silence to the Featherington farm, his mind plagued with doubts and an equal number of questions. Even during the excited, teary reunion with the child's parents and as the paramedics arrived to take the child to the hospital, Albert was quiet, distant. He could feel Shirley watching. She had always been quick to spot his moods.

"You should be happy, you know. You're a hero," she said moments after they returned to the highway.

He shrugged and let his eyes turn briefly to her.

"This is too real. I've never had a dream like this. I'm either in one helluva coma or dead, and this is a poor man's heaven."

His wife grimaced.

"Why do you keep saying you're dreaming?"

Albert looked at Shirley, at her beautiful face, the graceful lines of her body and wondered, if he could rescue little Alice Featherington in his dreams, could he prevent Shirley from dying? Could he?

"You died, you know," he said quietly, keeping his eyes clear and focused on the road as they entered the town's outskirts.

"Al? Why are you saying this?" The distress in her voice was real, *too* real for a simple dream.

"It's true. You have three lumps in your right breast. You don't check yourself for such things 'cause you think you're too young, but you'll find them in about four years from now, and it'll be too late. The cancer will have spread to your liver and lungs by then, and …."

He looked away, choking back the familiar emotions

that came with remembering her death.

"Albert! Why are you doing this?"

He turned the vehicle down their street.

"Because it's true."

"In your dream?"

"This is my dream, and it did happen. I knew where the Featherington girl was because it *did* happen—twenty years ago. And, fourteen years ago, you died, then Benny got killed in Afghanistan, and I've been alone ever since."

He parked the truck in their driveway and killed the motor. They sat in silence, Albert staring ahead at the house he and Benny were in the middle of painting. He could sense Shirley's gaze was hard on his face. This had been one hell of a dream, but now he wanted to wake up. It wasn't fun anymore.

A sound caused him to turn his head. Shirley's hands were under her sweater. She was kneading and poking her right breast. He watched her and began to smile. Maybe the dream wasn't so bad after all, and perhaps he could change his future, their future—in the dream at least.

"Lower," he said.

"Where?" She shot the question at him, her voice edgy.

"Lower. Further, toward your side. They're in a diagonal row."

He reached over and moved one of her hands.

"Oh my God," she gasped. "I can feel them. They're tiny."

He nodded, and their eyes met, and she began to cry.

"I don't understand," she said as he pulled her to him.

"It's just a dream, babe. Only this time, I can make it all better. I saved the Featherington kid, and now I can save you and," he choked back a sob, "and Benny."

They cried, shedding tears between kisses and desperate hugs. Albert was feeling remarkably happy. This was one hell of a fantastic dream.

Or was it?

He didn't know, and quite frankly, he didn't care.

Note: *A Prairie Yarn - This story is based on a dream I had, which I then spun into this little yarn. The concept of the story is universal and certainly not original. We all would love to travel back in time and change the things we regret or wish hadn't happened.*

8. THE OLD MAN

FRANKLIN, A CO-WORKER OF MINE, told me about the old man.

"You gotta see him," I was informed. At which point I found myself on the receiving end of gossip directed at the craggy-faced steam engineer who occasionally entered our world from the bowl of our office building to do whatever it was he did. I never noticed him much; I just knew he kept to himself.

"There's nothing strange about taking a lunch break outside," I replied.

"Not like this, man," Franklin exclaimed while circling a finger around his ear. "People say he's been doing the same weird thing for years."

At noon I took my lunch bag, left the building and found the old man exactly where my co-worker said he went every noon hour. It wasn't far, just a few steps away around the corner of the building. He stood at the edge of the wide sidewalk that ran outside our office building.

He was wearing a dark wool coat that could have easily belonged to one of the street people that bummed spare change along the avenue. An equally old toque graced his thinning scalp protecting him from the mid-February chill. He stood facing the sun, eyes closed, slowly peeling a navel orange, which he ate just as slowly, segment by segment.

I found a spot on a cold bench several feet from him and ate my meal, blowing on my chilled fingers in between bites. I realized then that I had seen him there many times before but had thought nothing of it. I had always been briskly going somewhere, and he was far enough out of the flow of pedestrians to be unnoticed by me.

About thirty minutes into my silent observation of him, he opened his eyes, placed the peels of his orange into a frayed side pocket and walked back to the office building.

I was curious, but not overly so. People have their rituals, especially during long and cold Canadian winters. Still, I was curious as to his reason for this particular ritual.

For the rest of the week, I made a point of timing my lunch break so I could follow him out into the cold. He was consistent, if anything. He never deviated and never ate any other fruit, just a large navel orange, while standing, facing the sun that struggled to rise in the winter sky. I watched him while I sat on my bench, shivering through a half-frozen bologna sandwich or leftover lasagna from the night before.

By Friday, I'd mustered enough courage to approach the old man. I stood quietly beside him and was about to touch his elbow when he turned his creased face to mine and, with eyes unopened, spoke.

"Bet yer wonderin' what I'm doing?"

He caught me completely off guard. I fumbled over the beginnings of an apology, but he rescued me.

"'S'alright young fella. Been asked that ques'ion a hun'erd times."

He turned his face back to the sun.

"Been doin' this mosta' my life, in one place or another."

I was about to quietly step away and leave him in peace when he continued.

"My dad came from Californi' for the big rush in '98 and darn near passed away from lack o' vitamins and sunlight. Took up gittin' his health from oranges he traded fer his gold. Kinda liked to eat 'em while soakin' up the sun. Reminded him o' home."

He took a thoughtful bite from one of his orange segments.

"Taught me the same, my dad."

Then he turned to me again and opened his eyes. They were a faded blue, with flecks of age and wisdom in them.

"Real relaxin'. You should try it."

That was it. He said no more, and I could think of nothing else that needed asking.

I joined him the next day.

Three of us now stand with the old man during the long sun-deprived winter months, "soakin' up the sun."

Note: The Old Man - This story is based on an older man, who did stand outside the building he worked in during the winter months to get, as he once offered to me, his quota of vitamin D and C.

9. GIRL ON A BUS

I SAW HER ON THE BUS. A weary traveller. Alone.

I have no idea how long I may have sat across from her before I happened to focus on her face and was moved by the kindred loneliness I felt in those eyes.

We don't even take the same bus.

I wait at the Ogilvie depot for the 5:15 to Riverdale. She leaves that bus at the rear when it arrives to deposit its passengers for the waiting connection to Porter Creek. I enter the front doors of the bus that she had just exited. Sometimes I see her disembodied head bouncing hurriedly past the windows as I make my way to my seat, but we never meet.

Except at the traffic lights on 2nd Avenue.

It was like that the first time we took notice of each other. Our buses pulled away from the depot, coming to a stop, side by side at the lights. Hers is waiting to turn right, and mine is in the turning lane to go left. For a brief moment, we sit across from each other, separated by glass, steel and the entire universe.

The day we met was early December, and the temperature was frigid, hovering in the minus 20s. She was in one of the newer, better-heated buses while I was in the older, less well-heated bus. The previous passenger of my seat had cleared a small circle of ice from the window with their breath to peer out into the frozen world, I supposed. The bus jerked to a stop. Distracted, I turned my head toward a flicker of motion that caught my attention—her bus.

She was right there beside me, just mere feet away. There was very little frost on her window. I could have touched her had I not been separated by the boundaries of our two worlds. As if sensing my gaze, she turned her face to mine. She had large dark eyes and smooth hair, the colour of those eyes. She was my age, I guessed. And, she was alone.

She smiled. She smiled, and suddenly my world included someone beyond myself. Then the bus lurched, and she was gone.

I don't know why she smiled. We are strangers. Then I realized that she could probably only see my eye through the circle of melted ice and frost. She had smiled at an eye.

It was Friday evening. In the stifling aloneness of my apartment, I thought of her throughout the weekend. I ride the bus out of necessity, and like most passengers, I pretend it is a solitary journey. My eyes fix on a narrow corridor, and I wait for the trip to end. I am alone. I do not talk. Others do not venture into conversation with me.

She was there on Monday evening, at the traffic lights. She sat in the same seat as before. There was less frost on my window, so I took a chance and looked, hoping to catch her eye. She stared blankly ahead, unaware of my hopeful gaze. She never saw me, never turned her head. Our communion last Friday had not been shared. I felt like a fool and slid back into the abyss of my isolation.

On Tuesday, she looked and smiled. I think she recognized my eye. My heart sat upright. There was hope.

Wednesday. Both our heads turned. Mine with a furtive glance, but she caught my eye, and we smiled in unison. It had become a game. We were strangers that shared a common orbit around our transportation and perhaps our loneliness.

On Thursday, the light at the intersection was already green, and I only saw her as our buses wrenched us apart. She had turned to look over her shoulder. To look at me!

She was looking for me!

Friday. She waved, smiled, and waved again—a fragile gift from a graceful black-gloved hand.

We have met this way almost every work day for the past three months. A fleeting moment of repose in the sea of mind-numbing sameness that is life on public transit. Once, she fell sick and disappeared for several days. I began to fear that she had perhaps moved, but then she returned, warming my heart with her smile, lifting a Kleenex to her flushed, petite nose as my bus lumbered away, leaving only a memory of her longed-for smile.

A smile. A wave. That's how it went. We mouthed a "Merry Christmas," and I wondered who gave her presents. The New Year came, the terrible, bone-chilling cold of January, but we never truly met. We never tried to share our names. We didn't take that plunge, content to remain safely anonymous behind our thin panes of separation.

Four days ago, I pressed a small, white cardboard sign to my window as we stopped at the lights. I'd written "Meet me?" on it.

I had wrestled with this for several days. Should I? Would it breach the unspoken limits of our casual friendship? Did I dare attempt to break through the human-made wall between us? Maybe she already had someone in her life. I didn't think so, however. She appeared to be as alone as I was. The anticipation of our daily encounters was mutual, I hoped.

The next day she held her own sign to the glass of her bus.

"Where? When?"

Her eyes were alive with expectancy. I caught a glimpse of delicate hand-drawn flowers on the sign's corners before she was pulled away from me. It had started. We had taken the next tentative step.

Where to meet? I was suddenly gripped by fear. I didn't really know her. She didn't know me, but lonely people take chances. What does she like to do? I know she likes to read. She had held up a copy of a Len Deighton novel as we passed one day. I had read the same book.

Suddenly I knew where to meet. The library. It was safe and very public. It wasn't overly romantic but a good start for two uncertain hearts.

"Tomorrow. at 6 p.m. Library." My sign instructed in big, bold fearless letters the next day.

Her smile flashed reassuringly, happy, as she nodded her head and then mouthed a vigorous "yes" to me. Then she was gone, the promise from her lips imprinted on my pounding heart.

Tomorrow, I finally meet the girl on the bus.

I hope she likes the man she finds on this side of the glass.

Note: Girl on a Bus - When I lived in Whitehorse, Yukon, I often rode city transit to my job at the Yukon News. During the long, cold days of winter, I would sometimes sit in a seat whose previous occupant had cleared a tennis ball-sized circle on the iced-over window, probably with the heel of their hand. This little portal offered me, and whomever else sat there, a tiny view of the wintery world that sped by.

10. BABY ON THE SIDEWALK

HEAT RADIATED OFF THE PARKING LOT in cruel sheets of stifling agony, hitting me like a blast furnace as I exited the sliding doors of the air-conditioned grocery store. I stopped at the edge of the wide sidewalk that flanked the building's front, and looked down at the yellow line painted along the curb, a reminder of the delineation between flesh and blood and moving steel and plastic. I looked up, feeling the exasperation of rush-hour shopping, and gazed furtively out at the multi-coloured sea of vehicles.

Where had I parked?

I saw the baby. It was sitting alone on a well-worn stretch of the sidewalk some distance to my left near one of those shopping cart corrals. The child had the delicate features of a girl. Her smooth baby face was crowned with a flurry of dark curls. She couldn't have been more than a year old and sat hunched over like an old man. She was clothed only in a white, disposable diaper.

I am not generally given to impulses. Carla often reminds me that I'm a schedule fanatic, but, being a father, I felt something of a twinge of paternal responsibility pull at my heart. I shifted my bag of groceries from one hand to the other and walked tentatively toward the child. As I approached, I could see that her left hand held tiny pebbles, which she was grinding fiercely, some slipping between her short, puffy fingers. Her other hand had a rattle, which she was driving with each downward swing onto the sunbaked concrete between her pale chubby legs. The movement seemed oddly precise and deliberate, and I wondered why the toy hadn't shattered into pieces.

It was troubling to see this child, any child, left unattended. I looked about for a parent, as I increased my pace toward her and suddenly noticed that my car was parked not far away. At that moment, I decided to change course and mind my own business and would have had I not felt so gripped by the child's apparent emotional distress.

Shielding my eyes from the glare of the evening sun, I stopped, casting my searching gaze further. Logic would suggest that there must be someone frantically looking for this misplaced child, but no one seemed to notice. How could anyone leave a helpless child sitting alone, half naked at a busy shopping complex?

Exasperated, I called to a group of young women standing near my vehicle. They were involved in an animated conversation and didn't hear me. I called again, allowing the frustration I felt to raise the volume of my voice. One of the women, dark-haired and noticeably annoyed at being interrupted, turned to squint at me and followed the line of my pointing arm to the baby. She gave me a shrug and turned away.

Perturbed and feeling the weariness from a day of sycophantic nonsense at my office, Carla was expecting me promptly home at seven, I advanced to the child and placed my groceries beside her. Squatting down, I reached for one of her hands. She responded to my presence and raised her face to mine. A piteous cry escaped her lips.

Our eyes met.

I caught my breath sharply. Those eyes, there was an unexpected presence in her dark eyes that clawed its way into my mind. Something vastly out of place compared to the innocence of her tender age was digging into my subconscious mind, suddenly unearthing a long-forgotten memory. I leaned closer as the sun beat mercilessly down upon us. I was transfixed, frozen, unable to move, as my skin crawled with the peculiar sensation that I might be the fly caught in a spider's web.

The memory of a bedroom closet rose out of the murky depths where it had been deliberately buried long ago. The closet's door would swing open of its own accord, whether by a draft or an inconsistency in the flooring or a latch that had grown flimsy with use, I would never know. Still, it revealed a black and seemingly fathomless interior, which unleashed unimaginable horrors for a young boy's imagination. Unwanted and unexpected, this memory materialized like a summer squall across my mind. I had laid awake in wide-eyed terror night after night, peering over the covers, staring at the open door of this dark chasm, conjuring up images of flesh-wrenching monsters in my adolescent imagination. Time and again, I had pushed the door shut before turning off the lamp next to my bed, but the door always swung open moments after I had cocooned myself in my blankets.

Click.

Creak.

It would creep open, and I would slowly lift the covers to witness what I was sure would be some foul instrument of my death swiftly approaching my bed.

The hellish, imagined evils of that closet seemed to reach out into my bedroom in a twisted dance, its tenebrous partner the shadowy flickers on the wall from the moonlit, wind-blown trees just outside my bedroom window. They reached for me, the closet and the shadows, reaching for my soul. I would sob loudly until my mother came and shamed me for my fear.

I swallowed hard, my mouth was suddenly pasty and dry.

A rivulet of sweat etched a searing trail down the edge of my cheek. My world focused on a rapidly narrowing tunnel flooding with the strange dark terror her eyes invoked. She penetrated my being with frightening ease, wrenching this hateful memory from its carefully crafted hiding spot. I pulled my trembling hand away from hers and tried to wipe the fear away, the bristles of my face rasping in my ears like sandpaper. For a moment, I knelt like that, held, captured, blinking profusely from the sting of sweat in my eyes, desperately trying to pull away.

I was looking into that closet again.

She shook with a sob: my God, those eyes.

My legs ached from squatting.

"Hey," I finally managed to whisper, "where's your mommy?"

I stood then, my knees popping in protest. My whole body was trembling, struck with this unexpected fear. I fought to rid myself of the sudden assault of emotions and looked about again. There was still no interest in the baby on the sidewalk. People with their laden bags passed us on all sides, their eyes and minds set on predetermined destinations that did not include a moment of shared concern. I was immediately angered. I, too had somewhere to be. Carla was expecting me, and I was always punctual.

I looked down at the child, her eyes had not left my face, and I could not walk away.

Sighing loudly, half hoping someone would hear my projected annoyance, I gently picked her up with my right arm and hooked my bag of groceries with my left hand. I purposely did not look down at her, even when she fearlessly snuggled up to my chest, nestling her head just under my chin. At least her diaper didn't feel soiled. I swallowed hard, wishing I had taken the time to wipe the salt from my stinging eyes and walked back to the main entrance.

I had to do something. I couldn't just leave her there, I told myself. Someone in customer service would know what to do.

Carla would have to live with that.

"Oh, you found her!" It was more of a statement than an exclamation of relief.

"W-what?" I managed to stutter as I placed my disturbing discovery on the edge of the courtesy counter. I let my bag of groceries slip carefully to the floor by my feet. The baby clung to me.

"You found the baby!"

She said this with a big, toothy smile.

The clerk had that disconcerting way of ending each sentence with a perky rise in intonation as if every comment spoke had to end in a question. The blue-streaked ponytail on the back of her head bounced in unison with each syllable as she spoke. I was immediately filled with trepidation.

"' Found? The baby?'" I echoed, letting my words grow edgy with the irritation I felt within me. I still did not understand.

The bounce stopped.

No smile.

"Yes, the baby."

Jerk, I thought to myself. She's just a kid herself.

"Look, I'm sorry. I need to get home, and you seem to know something about this kid."

I gently touched the baby's naked back. She was warm, sticky, and insisted on reaching a small arm underneath my jacket to grab a hand full of my damp shirt.

"I found her all alone," I continued, "just sitting out there."

Her smile returned with a raise of her eyebrows and a big bob of her head.

"Oh, I know."

"You know?" I tried to respond as calmly as possible.

"Uh-huh," she answered cheerfully.

Her mouth morphed into that vast, full smile again.

I grimaced and bit down on my lower lip.

"You act like this happens every day."

I could feel my frustration crawling out from the depths of my weariness. I levelled a shaky finger at her, but she, Phyllis, according to the plastic green, trimmed name tag on her green t-shirt, interrupted me with an even larger dimpled grin.

"Well, it does, you know."

"What does?" My arm finger in mid gesture.

"It happens every day," she answered, "seven o'clock. Someone brings the baby in, mostly every day. She's such a little cutie, isn't she?"

She leaned into the wide countertop and played with a strand of the child's dark hair.

"I've seen her, oh say, maybe five times now. Haven't I, you pretty little thing?"

The 'pretty little thing' pulled her head from my chest and eyed Phyllis.

"Oh, those eyes are something else, eh? Gee. I remember the—"

I cut her perky chatter off this time. "Wait just a minute. You mean to tell me her parents—"

"Mother."

"Okay, mother," I resumed pointing in exasperation at her, "her mother leaves her at the mall?"

I paused, and Phyllis nodded a vigorous yes.

I continued.

"Every evening at seven and leaves her baby out there?" I pointed ambiguously in the general direction of the parking lot.

"No."

I felt my eyes bulging and brought my hand down on the countertop with a slap of frustration that turned a few heads around us. Phyllis started and jumped back. The baby leaned into my chest, and gave her rattle a little shake, seeming oblivious to the discussion of her plight.

"But you just said...."

I groaned louder than was warranted and let my eyes fall shut. I did not need this. Give me someone from this planet to tell me what to do. I could sense time swiftly marching past seven. I raised my pleading eyes to the young woman.

Phyllis adjusted her green skirt, placed an elbow on the counter between us, rested her chin in the palm of her hand and looked at me with earnest seriousness.

"Her mom's not well, you know," she said, nodding, her eyebrows rising conspiratorial as if sharing some rich piece of gossip, her jaw bouncing up and down in her palm.

"Says an angel comes every night at seven and drops her little kid right there," she jabbed her other thumb vaguely in the direction of the parking lot, "on the curb, by the carts."

I stared at Phyllis, unsure of what to say. This was getting more bizarre by the moment.

"Doesn't family services do anything?" I finally asked.

She shook her head slowly, frowning.

"Nothing, yet."

"That doesn't make sense."

Phyllis nodded in agreement, her ponytail also nodding in agreement.

"What happens to her then?" I asked, holding my warm package closer. The child leaned into my chest. It felt strangely good.

Suddenly I was not in a hurry. Carla could wait, plus the air conditioning in the store was slowly reducing the heat-induced throbbing in my temples to a mild annoyance.

Phyllis smiled in her perky annoying way, shrugged minutely and sighed deeply through her slightly upturned nose. "I've taken her home a few times."

There was a hint of something almost dreamy in her voice as she said this. It puzzled me.

"You? Aren't you a little, uh, young?"

"Not really," she replied with only a slight hint of annoyance.

"Then there's Chuck," she continued, "the security guard, or Herb. One of them will take her home sometimes."

She stood back from the counter and pointed her thumb at the door behind and to the left of her. There was a big yellow happy face above Herb's nameplate.

"The manager, you know, sometimes takes her home or back to her mom."

"What's her mother's name?"

"'Lizabeth something."

She shrugged again like it was never really important to her.

"Where does 'Lizabeth something' live?"

"Crosstown. Near the Safeway on Fourth."

"What's her name?" I placed a hand on the side of the child's head. She snuggled, whimpering a tiny sound, like a kitten's purr. A delicate hand reached up to blindly feel the side of my face.

Oh, great.

Phyllis did her little smile and shrug thing again, not answering me.

"Should I call Herb or—" she smiled playfully, "do you want to take her home?"

I said yes to the first and no to the second. She shrugged and reached beneath the counter to bring up a green-coloured telephone receiver.

I was feeling confused. This situation was morally wrong on so many levels. The little hand at the side of my face found an eye, so I gently brought her fingers back down to my chest. She amused herself with my wrinkled tie. There was something nice and comforting about how she held onto me. The ghost of a memory flickered before me, and I thought of Colleen when she was this age. It was a good age. The age when they still needed you, even if only for a diaper change and a full bottle. I smiled and suddenly realized the day's weight had become a mere echo. This mysterious child who had dredged such dark and long-forgotten memories from within me was somehow entwining my mundane life with the strangeness of hers.

"Herb," Phyllis spoke into the receiver, "courtesy counter, please."

Her words echoed throughout the store over tinny-sounding ceiling speakers. She looked at me, her lips a fine line, carefully groomed eyebrows raised, then stood on her toes and gazed around what was visible of the store from where we were.

We waited.

And waited.

I mimicked her store surveillance although I had no idea what Herb looked like.

It was then that I suddenly realized my heart was pounding. The unconscious unthinkable thing that was trying to escape into my awareness filled my chest with nervous excitement. Several little streams of perspiration worked their way down the line of my jaw as memories of Colleen as a baby tumbled across my mind. Colleen was safe, with parents who were not perfect but cared and were there for her. Someone had to care for this baby. Someone had to.

No!

Not me!

I felt the warmth of this unusual but defenceless child against me. For some unknown reason, she had reached out to me in trust, and despite the frightening memory that had unexpectedly been pried from my childhood, for the first time in a long while, I felt needed. Carla had her house and a part-time property manager position, and Colleen had her loud music and boyfriends. I had my job, relentlessly the same and efficiently boring but a long way from making any kind of lasting impact on anything worthwhile.

No, continuing this unrealistic and painful train of thought made no sense. There was nothing I could do. I am not a social worker, and it had been many years since we had cared for a baby in the house.

"Maybe call that security guard," I ventured somewhat reluctantly.

Phyllis gave an annoyed sniff. Looking somewhat exasperated, she picked up the receiver again.

"Look, mister, you don't get it. People usually just take the kid home or leave her here, and we—"

"Just call what's his name, please."

I had to end this, I had to know the baby would be safe and taken care of. What was clamouring loudly at the edge of my consciousness was unthinkable, and illogical, and I needed to leave before—

"Chuck," she spoke into the headset.

"No, wait!" I spat it out so forcefully that she dropped the phone, and sharp rasping feedback screeched through the store. People turned to look.

"I'll take her home."

Stop.

What am I doing?

Stop. Stop.

I was already out the sliding doors, baby in arms.

Groceries?

Groceries!

No way was I going back now. I threw a quick, almost guilty glance over my shoulder. Phyllis was placing the receiver back under the counter, a huge smile on her face, like she knew something I didn't. That worried me. Maybe she was just relieved to see that someone other than her or Herb, or whatever that other guy's name was, was going to do something about the child, at least for the night. Maybe that's what she was thinking. Maybe.

The baby giggled in my arms.

Carla was going to flip.

Carla did not flip.

I should have called from the car and warned her, but what could I possibly say that didn't make me sound like a crazy person? I'm not rash; I appreciate routine; I have been called boringly habitual, but what I was doing was definitely heedless. How could I explain this to her?

I parked the car in the back alley behind the garage, out of sight, and slipped into the house through the rear entrance, the baby held tightly to me. The hinges of the screen door screeched like fingernails across a blackboard. I had been meaning to fix that. Carla heard it.

"Harold?"

Carla was in the kitchen, just off the ample back porch. I heard a rattle of utensils, and very suddenly, she was there, standing in the hallway, dishtowel in her hands. It was part of a set I'd given her at Christmas. They were hand embroidered and very expensive. She was happy then. She was not happy now. I was unusually late, and her fair complexion had darkened into a threatening cloud that matched the shiny blackness of her carefully curled hair. Threatening, that is, until she saw the baby in my arms. Her perfect eyebrows shot up, and her mouth opened in a wide-mouthed and happy smile. I swallowed hard and began my pre-rehearsed attempt at an explanation.

"A baby!" She squealed with a girlish glee. I had not heard from her in many years. The words sounded very strange within these walls. With deft skill, she flicked the dishtowel over her left shoulder and just as quickly relieved me of my little bundle. My arms ached.

"Uh, Carla," I started, but she was off, around the corner to the kitchen, making cute cooing sounds to the child.

What? She seemed overwhelmed with joy. I dragged my coat off, throwing it haphazardly into the closet. Hang it up later.

"Carla," I protested, hoping I didn't sound too harsh. She seemed pretty happy… but… well, the kid was my responsibility. I'd found her. She was technically my problem.

I came around the corner into our small, brightly lit kitchen. The table was set for the evening meal, and the air was rich with the aroma of pot roast—my favourite. A woozy nagging in the pit of my stomach reminded me that I was feeling famished. Reaching for a carrot stick from the table and brandishing it like a sword, I turned to where Carla was leaning against the counter by the sink. I was ready to defend my choice to bring the child home. This baby was my problem. The baby—

I stopped abruptly, my heels squeaking on the linoleum. My mouth dropped open involuntarily. The carrot fell from my suddenly trembling hands and spiralled down to the floor. A part of my brain heard it hit the floor with a tiny thud.

Carla was not holding a baby in a cloth diaper.

She held a child of four or five in her arms, dressed in a blue cotton gingham skirt with crinolines and puffy sleeves that stopped just short of her elbows. There were white socks, shiny black shoes with silver buckles on what should have been pudgy bare feet, and a white knitted bow in what were now quite long dark brown tresses. She still held onto the rattle.

"Oh, Harold. A little girl!" Carla stopped cuddling and squeezing the baby—child—long enough to flash me what looked like a grateful smile.

Was I going insane? I glanced around the kitchen for the baby. No baby. What was going on here? Where was the baby?

I opened my mouth to speak but could not. My lips felt like sticky leather, and the taste of fear sat on my tongue like a stone gargoyle as a realization gripped me. The closet of my horrors loomed ominously in front of me, and I began to feel my chest constrict again. I wanted to run, to hide, to reach some safe shore of sanity, but it held me captive as the infant slowly turned her head to me. Her eyes smiled at me, and they reached into me as effortlessly as they had at the grocery store parking lot. They ripped me from reality and sucked me into my long-buried terror. I fought, coughed, my throat dry like sawdust, and I jerked my eyes away as if a hot poker threatened them.

"Carla," I managed to gasp as I lunged across the kitchen floor, keeping my eyes averted. My foot found the fallen carrot, and it crunched loudly and sharply as it rocketed out from the sides of my shoe.

"Oh, Harold."

She ignored me.

"Where did you find her? Who is she? What's her name?"

Her barrage of questions was a cacophonous jumble of unintelligible sounds in my head as I pulled the child roughly from her arms. Perhaps a little too roughly. I swung the girl around, and the rattle shook. She was heavier and smelled of flowers. I forced myself to face those fathomless eyes.

"What happened here? Who are you?" I demanded fiercely, resisting the panic rushing with a volcanic vengeance up my throat.

Her lashes were long and delicate, and her large dark eyes blinked at me. She squirmed in my too-hard grip and answered with a surprisingly firm adult tone to her voice.

"Pama," she said through tiny white and clenched teeth.

I nearly dropped her.

Carla would not listen to my rattled explanation. She took Pama from me, reproving me sternly for unseemly behaviour towards her "little angel." Using grand angry gestures, I explained several times that I had brought home a baby from the grocery store. I found her, I said, not a four-year-old dressed in her Sunday best but a near-naked baby. Wasn't it a baby that she had taken from my arms? Yes, I sputtered in answer to my question, it was a baby.

A. Little. Baby.

I explained to her what Phyllis at the courtesy counter had told me about 'Lizabeth or something, her unwell mother, but I might as well have been talking to a wall. I paced the kitchen floor feeling like the great patriarchal protector of my family but looking very much like an emotionally disturbed man, barking and waving my arms.

She ignored me, and with a touch of motherly tenderness I had not seen for many years, she sat Pama at the table, lovingly lifting the thickness of her hair so that it lay across her young shoulders.

"You've had a trying day, dear." Carla dismissed me, "No more nonsense. Now go and wash up, and we'll have dinner with Pama. Oh, isn't she so sweet?"

She smiled cutely, physically shooing me out of the kitchen and towards the hallway.

Pama just smiled and giggled, looking entirely too comfortable. She seemed to belong like this was her home, and Carla was her mother. An ominous shiver traversed the hair at the back of my neck as I closed the bathroom door behind me.

I stood facing the vanity for a full five minutes, my fingers attempting to gouge into the sides of the countertop. My face, haggard and drawn from the rush of emotions, stared back at me from the mirror. I had to think this through. None of what had just happened made any sense. It was like a terrible dream. Maybe it was.

My eyes were bloodshot and my cheeks flushed with emotion. I did look a mess. I reached a shaking hand up to my face, felt the aging contours of my jaw, and slid it through my dishevelled hair. My fingers found the ridge of the scar that ran two inches along my part—the tree. I had tried to chop that terrifying tree down outside my bedroom window. I had awakened in the hospital some hours later to the vision of my mother's concerned yet angry face. My parents had moved me to the basement bedroom after that, where even further unimaginable terrors awaited me.

I hoped that I would be waking up any minute.

I filled the basin with scolding water, and washed my face with a cloth letting the heat soothe my tense muscles and then ran a comb through my hair. I felt lost. The situation was out of control. Hadn't others taken this child home before me? Phyllis at the store had said so. Did this bizarre transformation from helpless babe to precocious child happen before their eyes? Why was this happening to me? Why didn't Carla see the change in the baby? This was Twilight Zone material. God, what was I going to do? My brain ached.

Carla called from the kitchen with that tone in her voice. I hated that tone; it made me feel like a child. I grabbed the door handle and stopped. I was a Good Samaritan when I rescued the baby from the sidewalk. Or had I rescued her? Perhaps, she was rescuing us from our dull lives. Carla was happy—happier than I had seen her in years. I was used to her efficient self-control. She rarely laughed anymore. Our lives had become routine, each of us settling into what were the easiest roles to maintain the normalcy of a middle-aged couple with a teenage child. Everything had been fine until I picked up the baby on the sidewalk. But now, I was feeling completely freaked out. Curious too, but my stomach was churning with the fear of the unknown—none of this made sense. I did bring a baby home. I did, didn't I?

I shook my head, sighing heavily through my mouth, and Carla called again. Okay, reality check, let's get some answers. Go out there and get some answers. I walked into the hall and purposefully entered the kitchen. Carla was sitting at her place, with her back to the refrigerator door, looking a trifle annoyed at me. Our mysterious guest was sitting where Colleen usually sat. Where was Colleen? I was about to ask that question when I choked on the saliva in my throat.

Pama was no longer a four-year-old. She now appeared to be at least ten, and the blue gingham dress had "grown" lace ruffles around the neck and arms and seemed to fit her larger size perfectly. Like the dress had been tailored to fit. Her knitted hair bow now clasped the side of her head and had shiny little pearls sown around its crimped edges. It held several long and healthy-looking ringlets of hair in place while the rest hung pleasantly down and over her shoulders. I could not see her shoes, for they were hidden beneath the table, but I could imagine the changes that had occurred while I was in the washroom had also extended to her feet.

I stumbled forward like someone trapped in a reoccurring nightmare. I wanted so badly to run and scream and slap myself and wake up. But I could not. I slid slowly and deliberately down into my chair, watching Pama. She seemed very normal. I could see nothing extraordinary about her except for those eyes. They still played with your soul like a hot wind on chimes.

Carla was speaking.

"Harold? Harold?"

I turned my gaze to her, not wanting to take my eyes off Pama. Each moment was beginning to carry a surreal weight.

"Um?"

"How many slices?"

What was she talking about? I shifted my eyes to Pama and asked my question, directed at Carla. "When did this happen? Did you see it happen?"

I think Carla just stared at me, for when she did not answer, I looked at her and saw her what-kind-of-an-idiot-question-is-that frown.

"When did this child become a, uh, you know, one of those tween kids?" I said my words very slowly, bringing my eyes cautiously back to the girl. Deliberate. I could feel my teeth grinding as she lifted her eyes to mine. I was feeling bold and confrontational.

Pama smiled and reached for her glass of milk. The rattle, blue and looking aged, lay beside her plate. I could not see any pebbles she had been furiously holding onto when I'd first found her. Whoever or whatever she was, the fact that I alone could see the changes in her did not seem of interest to her.

"Excuse me?" Carla demanded.

I swallowed, audibly loud, "Carla, I brought home a baby girl in a diaper," my hands again began their dance through the air. "Suddenly, she is four or five and dressed like, like this. I go to the bathroom, and five minutes later, she is like—like this, ten, or something."

"Nine."

The girl's firm voice jolted me like an electric shock. "Oh, excuse me. I did not mean to interrupt."

She smiled shyly, her dimples and a milk moustache beneath her wickedly cute nose making her apology almost irresistibly endearing.

"Harold," Carla scolded, "what is wrong with you?"

My hand hit the table. My plate caught the force of the anger, and it and my fork flipped into the air and landed upside down with a clatter. Peas and mashed potatoes splattered against the wall beside me. I didn't care. Like steam rising through an iron grate, rage was finding its way through the cracks of my carefully held civility. I wanted answers.

"Carla," I growled, "listen to me. I brought home a baby. A baby, Carla!" I took a deep breath. My whole body was shaking. "There is something absolutely bizarre going on here, and you can't see it happening?"

I grabbed the girl's right arm and leaned into her from across the table.

"Who are you?"

For the first time, she appeared to be very frightened; tears filled her eyes and then ran like a torrent down the soft contours of her face. It had to be an act.

"Pama," she replied in a hushed tone, her face taut with distress.

Carla protested and grabbed my arm. I brushed her hand away.

"Pama? What, is that short for Pamela?"

Carla protested louder. Then, to my surprise, Pama's demeanour suddenly flipped from childish fear to a dark and threatening rage. She lowered her face, and those soulless eyes narrowed and laid me bare and unprotected again. I flinched, shocked, but did not let go of the child's arm. With what I can only describe as a strength vastly out of comparison to her age, she gripped my hand and pulled it from her arm, flinging it away like a piece of fuzz from a sweater. The force of the release caused me to jerk back down into my chair.

Then the little girl snatched her rattle from the table, its beads knocking about, clenched her other hand tightly and screamed shrilly at me, "My name is Pama!"

Then she sat up very straight, carefully placed the aged rattle back beside her plate, tilted her head a little to the left, smoothed out her dress around her lap and said quite gently with just a hint of an eternal seething bitterness, "My mother calls me Pamela."

Pama changed once more that evening, unabashedly right before my entire family.

I had recanted at the supper table, withdrawing into a sullen silence. What choice did I have? Carla could not see what I was seeing. I wanted to grab this demon in a child's skin and drag her back to the parking lot where I'd had the grave misfortune of being sucked into this insane nightmare.

Partway through the meal, Colleen arrived home through the back door from extracurricular volleyball practice, complaining loudly of some major emotional event in her life. Upon entering the kitchen, she proceeded to act as if she'd always known Pama.

The continuing madness unfolded like this: I heard the back door slam, followed by Colleen doing her usual after-school routine, grumbling, complaining, the my-life-sucks kind of nonsense. I hear her school bag thump on the hall floor, where she drops it a few feet from her bedroom door. I turn in my chair to follow her as she walks into the surreal atmosphere of the kitchen, me glowering as my feet twitch and tap on the floor while my hands drum out my ever-increasing fears in a staccato madman's jig on the table and Carla and Pama chatting it up like a loving mother and sweetheart daughter.

"Oh, hi, Pama," my daughter gushes. "Cute dress."

"Col!" This evil parasite exhales as she leaps up to hug my daughter. My mouth drops.

She hugged my daughter.

I nearly crawled out of my skin, but I managed to grip the hard, curved edges of the table and redirected my rage to that narrow point between flesh and wood. My fingers ached.

Colleen and Pama settled at the table, laughing and giggling as if they had been the dearest and closest friends since kindergarten. After she and Colleen cleaned up the kitchen, we all retreated to the family room in the basement, where this child, if that is what she is, asks explicitly to see our photo albums. Why our photos, I wondered? What did she need to know about my family? Without hesitation, Carla pulled a stack of albums from one of the bookcases, albums that we hadn't looked at in years. The last time we had sat as a family in the family room had been when we had hosted Carla's family's annual Christmas dinner, an event I loathed—about as much as a picnic on a hot summer day with wasps. That was about five years ago.

We simply did not do anything together anymore. Our evenings consisted of the same individual treks through the dark forests of inane sameness. Carla to her laptop and any property management business that might present itself, Colleen to her bedroom and whatever mysterious things she did there, and me to the den to shut my brain off from my life by watching hours of television. It's what we did, what we do, every night.

Pama's ability to comprehend and communicate seemed to have grown as she 'grew.' It was as if she really were a nine-year-old. I didn't believe it for one minute. She could fool Carla and Colleen, but I had found her. I knew her and saw clearly past the elaborate deception.

We had flipped to the pages that held photos of Colleens' last birthday party when Pama pointed to one image and asked what a particular item was in the picture. All three of us looked up at her at the same time. I watched her questioning face intently, blinked, and suddenly she was much older.

She changed from a nine-year-old to what appeared to be Colleen's age of fourteen, and only I seemed to notice. My daughter and Carla just kept on talking, flipping the pages. Carla even had to move a little on the couch to accommodate Pama's significantly larger size. It was as if her bizarre and fantastical change had not just happened before us all.

"Hold on," I croaked hoarsely, choking on what little saliva was trickling down my throat. "Didn't you see that? She just changed! Right here!"

I leapt to my feet, brandishing a finger at Pama.

"Right in front of us. Didn't anyone see that?"

No. No one had seen the transformation, and no one would answer any more of my 'ridiculous questions.' My family elected to ignore me, embracing this cute, demonic entity. Pama smiled, and my wife and daughter slowly succumbed to her Siren call. As the evening progressed, I was increasingly regarded with indifference. I should have been more than angry, I should have been ready to wrench every smooth limb from her evil body, but a macabre sense of curiosity held me at bay. I would follow this terrible nightmarish plot through and see what the end might be.

That thought made me shudder.

I sat quietly across from Carla and noted the change in our guest with forced silence. Pama had changed into a deceptively lovely young woman. A short sleeveless blouse shaded in angular patterns of blues with a neckline edged with little ruffles had replaced her gingham dress. She now wore tight-fitting blue jeans that seemed, as I half suspected as if they were designed for her. Her hair was long, slightly reddish, falling halfway down her back, and held tightly to the sides of her aquiline head by two tiny plastic blue bows. Her face was evenly tanned, having a hint of the woman she would possibly become. Her eyes, which occasionally flickered to touch mine with that disturbing sense of the dark closet of my childhood, still contained that mysterious feeling of maturity that didn't quite fit her age. Hanging from her graceful neck was a small, blue, and very old-looking miniature rattle.

My daughter laughed again. Laughed again? I hadn't heard her laugh in a very long time. It puzzled me that Colleen seemed so happy. It was as if Pama brought the child out of her again. She appeared to unearth something long covered over by teenage angst and the terse, cold disputes we often had. The two girls seemed to know each other as if they were life-long friends. Colleen would lean into Pama, whisper something as she pointed at a photo, and then they would laugh and giggle with an intimacy that inferred a historical friendship I knew was impossible. Pama had done something diabolical to my child's perception of reality, but I sighed begrudgingly; for the first time in a long time, my daughter sat with her family. She seemed almost human again. Not isolated in her room, listening to her loud boy band music, and having her infuriatingly long, secretive phone calls with boys that I knew she did not want me to meet.

My daughter was happy.

This was very confusing.

Even Carla laughed freely, the crowfeet betraying her age around her eyes fading with the laughter of forgotten memories as the three flipped page after page through my family history. A history that had once been painted with the vibrant colours of happiness, silliness and gaiety and a desire to be together. What had happened to us? How had we become so disparate from each other?

Then, I had calmed down enough and decided to bring out my digital camera. Indeed, I was somewhat angry for not thinking of this sooner, but I had been far too disturbed by the complete powerlessness I had felt this evening to think rationally. I had been caught in Pama's torrential flood of fear and emotional manipulation.

I shot several dozen images, hoping Pama would make one of her transformations, but she did not. Before each photo, she would wryly lift her eyes and look through the lens, like she knew I was about to photograph her. My sweaty hands would shake, my breath falter on my lips, and something deep inside begged to break away and crawl under the covers of my childhood fears, but I remained steadfast in my purpose to document one of her startling changes. She smiled, made lovely comments about one image or another in the albums, laughed with my wife and daughter and appeared sincerely happy as they shared intimate stories from our life. I was feeling more and more confused. What was this creature's purpose in my home? What terrible agenda did it have?

I would have taken a hundred more images, but as she flipped the last page of an album closed with a slap, Carla suddenly announced that it was far too late to look at any more photos.

She immediately shooed the two girls off to bed. Pama could share Colleens' bed. My heart leapt into my throat. I would not have my daughter sleeping in the same room with whatever I had brought home. Again, though, I was outnumbered. I argued furiously with Carla, running through my facts, my fears, and my theories, but to no avail. As it had been all night, my protests were met with firm resistance. Carla was adamant; she was as furious towards my rejection of Pama as I was towards her unnatural acceptance of our guest.

Colleen glared at me with an all too familiar contempt as she went to her room with Pama in tow.

Pama just smiled.

I hung my head, stomped around the house, and grumbled, but eventually found myself alone and exiled to the family room couch for the night.

I would not sleep.

How could I sleep?

Some alien thing had stolen the minds and hearts of my family.

Carla's gentle shaking woke me.

I sat up suddenly, the blood draining from my head with a Vesuvius roar that brought on an instant throbbing just behind my right eye. My lower back protested painfully from my night on the couch.

"You're late for work, Harold."

Her voice punched through my fog—God, what a dream.

Rubbing my forehead, I staggered to my feet, half sensing the pathetic condition of my clothes, and aimed in the general direction of the basement bathroom. Why didn't I have a shower last night?

"What time is it?" I muttered. "Did Colleen get off to school on time?"

"Eight thirty-one," Carla answered efficiently from somewhere. "Colleen left at seven forty-five to catch the bus with Pama. She's such a nice girl."

Pama!

Oh, God. I shuddered. A wave of dizziness swept over me, and I had to brace myself against the hallway wall. The bizarre events of last night had not been a dream!

Pama went to school; she went to my daughter's school!

Of course, somehow, it all made sense in my stressed mind. I keenly remembered her interest in our photo albums. That's when she changed that last time. Maybe, whatever kind of creature she was, fed off of—of what? Children? She would want to go to a school, to go after the children! That's what she was after! She had planned to go to school with Colleen all along, and I was the stupid, pathetic father that led her to my child. I had led her to children!

Idiot.

My life was spiralling out of my control, and I didn't like it. I felt like I was floundering in a growing vortex of madness. I had to get to Colleen's school and end this now!

In the washroom, I ran a comb through my thinning, confusion of hair and splashed cold water over the weary lines of my face. Visions of dead children began to flood my mind. I don't think Carla heard me rasp a goodbye as I exploded out the backdoor, but I didn't care. I seemed to be the only sane person left in my home.

I hastily called my office from my cell phone in the car and lied. I was sick. I had never missed a day of work due to illness, but my whole stupid world had become infected with a disease called Pama. All I knew and loved had been poisoned by a crafty shape-shifting creature that had possessed the hearts of my wife and daughter.

I hit the overpass, driving far more than the posted speed limit, narrowly missing a slow-moving delivery truck. It was usually a thirty-minute drive from the suburbs to Colleen's high school, it was already 9:25, and traffic was heavy. I drove like a madman, blasting my horn at otherwise civil drivers, taking chances I would never have dreamed of before, but I was a man possessed by a desperate need to regain control of my world and save my daughter. My carefully crafted middle-class life had been invaded, and nothing was normal anymore. For a moment, my actions frightened me. I was breaking every painstakingly created rule of my scheduled life, every sense of security and comfort I had carefully built. I could die at any moment. My life could be extinguished by the carelessness of another driver or by my desperate actions. I was racing towards the horrors that had patiently waited for me—just for me—night after night in the terrifying shadow of my closet. I'm not compulsive. I like order; I need structure and the assurance of sameness. Everything I know needs to stay the same. That was the only way to defeat what waited for me in that closet, by not making any sudden moves, by laying in the same position night after night. The shadows wouldn't see you that way; they won't find you and kill you then.

Oh God, Colleen. I hoped I wasn't too late.

As I dangerously careened into the school parking lot, I felt oddly alive, really alive and yet terrified to the murky depths of my awareness.

I leapt from the car and moved with incredible speed. Pushing through the front doors, past the surprised faces in the front office, and up two flights of stairs gleaming with institutional wax. My senses were quickened to the extreme; every second played out in mind-numbing clarity. I seemed to drift outside my body and watch from someplace far away and yet frighteningly near. I slipped and slammed ungracefully headfirst onto the second-floor landing and then into swinging doors marked with the fingerprints of countless children. Living children! I didn't stop. I propelled myself forward, arms and legs driven with a ferocity and desperation that felt no immediate sensation of pain.

The door marked 233 bursts open with the force of my fear as I suddenly found my mind imprisoned in my body, my chest heaving and straining for air, my eyes, the feel of anguish and hope in them, narrowed, focused, scanning, searching.

Where was she? By the windows—with Pama!

Colleen looks alive, unharmed. No bodies, no mangled, broken bodies, and no hellish demon wrenching the life from the children.

What?

Pama was still the same age as last night and still deceptively innocent.

No one is dead.

"May I help you?"

I stared at Pama. My face is taut with emotion; my eyes bulge with the pressure of my pounding, terrified heart. Colleen lifts her eyes to the sudden eruption of noise, smiles as she recognizes me, and then frowns just as quickly. The life of the classroom stops, and the universe waits.

"Excuse me?" A voice said from elsewhere.

Pama connects with my eyes. I see her smile, though my own eyes never leave hers. The hunter and the hunted. The soulless and the beguiled. I want to scream, wretch, throw myself to the floor and beg for release from this hell, but what shred of self-preservation I have left prevails, and I look away.

"Excuse me. May I help you, uh, Mr —?"

I focus on the voice, and see the face. I know her. Petite. Dark, mid-thirties. Colleen's teacher. A good teacher, I believe. A vague memory of a parent-teacher interview slips through my mind. Her name. Alisha Stinson. Miss Alisha Stinson.

"Harold. Harold Johnson, uh, Miss Stinson. I'm Colleen's father," I stammer, suddenly feeling unclothed and painfully self-aware.

I run a trembling hand through my hair and immediately sense discomfort in that hand. I'm aware of something wet oozing down my left leg in the outer edges of my thoughts. Am I bleeding?

"Mr. Johnson? Is there a problem?" Miss Stinson looks a little anxious. "Are you all right?"

"Uh, yeah," I reply as my eyes shift to Pama. Her dark eyes rend my soul into tattered shreds of whimpering fear. I tremble as if a cold breeze had just blown over me, "I—I just wanted to sit in on the class today."

"Really?" Miss Stinson's eyebrows arch up, clearly not convinced of any good intentions on my part.

I catch the look of disapproval in her eyes. I've never come before, but then, neither has Pama. "Look, I know it's kind of sudden, but I have the day off, and I thought it would be sort of nice to see what my daughter does, uh, all day." I shrugged. "You know, like when I'm at work."

It was a weak argument, and I must have looked like a down-on-his-luck street person begging for a handout.

Still, she suddenly smiled graciously, nodded her head and turned me to the class by the elbow, "Class, this is Colleen's father, Mr. Johnson, and he's going to spend some time with us this morning watching what we do."

Watching Pama, you mean, I thought, but then my brain deciphered what she'd said.

"Uh, no, I need to be here all day," I said, trying not to sound too desperate.

One of her eyebrows arched up.

"Really? All day? Why is that, Mr. Johnson?"

I looked at her, searching her face, my mind racing with hastily contrived excuses. I was positive she would know if I lied. So, I lied.

"Uh, I have the day off; I, uh, want to see why my daughter is such a, uh, good student."

My daughter's teacher sighed through her nose, her eyes never leaving my face. I began to squirm under the gaze of those penetrating eyes. It was clear that she was in charge here. I smiled a hopeful smile, trying to look sane.

"Very well, I trust you signed in at the front office when you entered the school?"

"Yes," I said, perhaps a little too hastily.

Her eyebrow shot up again, but she gestured for me to follow her and led me to an area in the back of the classroom where there were chairs, students' cubbyholes and a place to hang coats. Several students looked at me, appearing slightly alarmed.

"We're right in the middle of the second period, Mr. Johnson. Colleen's doing math. If you want, you may take one of these chairs and sit next to her and—"

"No."

I stopped her with a rush of adrenaline-driven emotion. Then smiled apologetically as she flinched. "I mean, I'll just sit here."

She started to turn away, a trace of confusion playing on her face, but I grabbed her arm. She stumbled as I pulled her close. "Tell me, do you know that girl over there?"

She looked at me, frowned, and then turned to see where I was shamelessly pointing. Pama had returned to her conversation with Colleen, who was throwing glances my way. She looked concerned. Or, it might have been anger in her eyes.

The teacher turned her eyes back to me.

"Do you mean Pama?"

"Yes, yes, her. Do you know her?"

The frown deepened. I must have appeared very odd, but I didn't care. "Yes," she slowly ventured, "as well as any of my students."

"She's a student of yours?" I hissed. Several heads turned in our direction.

"Yes, Mr. Johnson, she's been with us since September. Is there a problem?"

"Do you *really* know who she is?"

"Excuse me?"

"Pama. Do you know *what* she is?" I felt the blood rushing to my head; black spots flitted across my vision like rising ash from a dying campfire. The thirst for absolution from my fear was coursing through me again. Had this child duped the entire world? I knew I wasn't crazy.

"Mr. Johnson, you're hurting me."

I looked down. I was holding her arm tightly, and I was hurting her. I pushed her arm aside and leaned into her face. She scrunched her nose at the closeness of my breath. My teeth. I hadn't brushed my teeth.

"Listen. I don't think you know what you have here. I don't think she's human, and I think your entire class could be in grave danger. You should call the principal and evacuate the school. I think she's maybe an —" I caught the disbelieving look filling her eyes. "—uh, I don't know. Just get my daughter and the other students out of the—" I stopped, my arms in a mid sweep. Colleen's teacher had narrowed her eyes, and I suddenly felt naked. How did she do that?

"Mr. Johnson," she whispered sharply, "you had better be joking. Actually, no, you had better not be joking. I have a class to teach, and even though this is highly irregular, you may sit here and watch, but otherwise leave my students alone."

She turned to leave me there, my mouth still caught in mid-sentence. She stopped, reversed on her heels, put a small hand on my chest and forced me down into a chair. She leaned in close to my ear.

"Furthermore, Mr. Johnson, Pama is one of the brightest and most intelligent students I have ever had the privilege to teach. Your daughter is fortunate to have her as a friend and a mentor."

She smiled tightly, inches from my face, straightened up, smoothed her dress and finished me off like a skilled swordsman.

"Now sit there, watch the class and be quiet. Or, leave."

She walked away then, several students chuckling. My eyes flew to Colleen. She had seen and heard everything that had just transpired, and the apparent hope on her face for my removal from the classroom hung in the space between us like a scream.

I slumped back into the chair, resigned, and allowed my eyes to follow Miss Stinson to the front of her classroom. I couldn't believe it. I sighed heavily. Again, I felt outnumbered. Helpless.

I crossed my arms. I would just sit and watch the class. Watch Pama. I was no fool. If everybody else was drawn into her illusion, that was fine. I wouldn't be. I knew what she was.

I pulled my comb from my jacket pocket and felt the Swiss Army knife I always carried there.

I watched Colleen and Pama throughout the three remaining periods of the day. I followed them to the large lunchroom, where I sat off in a corner, my eyes never leaving. I followed them to gym class and watched as Pama ran laps with my daughter and then played a perfect game of volleyball. I followed them out onto the school grounds at break time, where I had to explain my presence to school staff, my eyes never leaving Pama even then. All through this, I could feel Colleen's confusion and anger over what I'm sure she had hoped would be a short fatherly intrusion.

Pama mostly ignored me, except when she would cast that soulless smile at me, freezing me with the disturbingly black depths of her eyes.

Whenever I could, I cornered students in her classes and quietly asked them if they knew Pama and how long they had known her. The answers were all the same; it was as if I was the only person who hadn't known her.

As the day progressed, a growing sense of confusion filled my mind. Was the entire school delusional? Pama continued to flash her engaging and manipulative smile to her fellow students while, with one glance, reminding me of the dark shadows of my fears. I had to close that closet door, but no one would listen to me. I had become the court jester, the clown of my nightmare. Word spread throughout the school as teachers and students alike would stroll past the open doors of the classroom, hoping to capture a glimpse of Colleen's strange father.

I didn't care. Pama was my concern. She, however, seemed to be the joyful focus of the class. She laughed and helped others, floating from one student to the next, often giving a hand to Miss Stinson and the English language teacher who joined her in the afternoon. Pama's smooth dance of joyful inclusion was a remarkable thing to watch. It reminded me of a black widow spider courting her unlucky mate. Grace, charm, a little romancing and then—dinner. Everywhere she went, she brought a sense of comfort and well-being. She was smart. She knew the answers to every question, not arrogantly, but with the deceptive gentleness of a wise old teacher. I was amazed. How gullible these young people were. Why could only I see through her trickery? Why wasn't I charmed by her evil and infectious persona? Could no one else sense the monster lurking in the shadowy depths of her eyes?

She had not changed once during the day, her bouncy positive attitude dancing around the room, infecting everybody with her lust for learning and her zeal for living. I remained distant, untouched, unmoved, more determined than ever to unmask her, to call her charade.

My head ached and throbbed by the time the final bell rang, and the class erupted into a chaos of shuffling books, scraping chairs and Miss Stinson giving last-minute homework assignments. I watched Pama. She and Colleen gathered their books together and would have left without even acknowledging my presence had I not reached for Colleen's arm. She froze, and I could sense the Everest of tension between us. Pama stopped and turned that lethally cute face towards me. I avoided her eyes.

"Colleen, I'll give you a ride home," I ordered. I knew she probably hated me right now, but I didn't care; I was saving her life.

My daughter pulled away from my hand and threw me an angry sideways glance.

"Not on your life, Dad. Come on, Pama."

"What? Wait a minute, Colleen." *What did she say?*

"Is Pama coming home again? With you? To my house?"

Miss Stinson was making her way toward me, but I caught up to Colleen and attempted to grab her arm again. She pulled away.

"Of course, Dad. She lives with us. We need to get to the bus."

"Mr. Johnson?"

My daughter, my little girl, was walking away from me with Pama. She lives with us? I had to stop this. I could feel the killing weight of the knife in my jacket. It would accomplish what needed to be done.

"Excuse me. Mr. Johnson?"

My head felt like it was ready to explode. I had been patient all day, watching, wondering, trying to hold onto my sanity's last fetters. Reasoning with myself, analyzing the events of the day before and today—trying to see past my deep sense of dread. She was the terror in my closet; this innocent-looking and sweet-acting girl was the horrible darkness in my closet. Why did this have to happen now? Why did she come to school? Something wasn't right. I had to figure this out. Figure out what, however? The answer seemed to elude me like sand slipping through my fingers.

"Mr. Johnson!"

"What?" I roared at the face that suddenly blocked my view of the departing girls.

She tensed with the severity of my response, but she was a teacher. She had stared down countless bullies before me.

"Sorry," I mumbled, feeling suddenly ashamed.

"Go home, Mr. Johnson. Get some rest. You need it." She turned to address a student near her but stopped. "Oh, and don't come here unannounced again. Clear any visit with the front office."

She didn't wait for my reply. Just left me standing in the middle of the ebbing flow of escaping students. My mouth was parched. I looked for Colleen and Pama, but they were gone.

I quickly made my way to the parking lot. My car was not there. In my furious haste to enter the school to save my child, I had parked in a handicap zone. It took me an hour and sixty-eight dollars to get to the city compound by taxi and another hour to get home through rush-hour traffic. This had been a terrible day. I almost wished that Pama would transform into something evil and rend me limb from limb, swallow every fetter of my torn and broken soul. I didn't care. I was hungry, confused, and weary from lack of sleep and feeling alone. More alone than I had ever felt before.

At 6:15, I stumbled through the back door of my home, its hinges screeching their unwelcome hello. I threw my jacket toward the closet, the knife thumping dully against the wall. I didn't care. Carla was in the kitchen, peeling carrots. Didn't we have carrots last night?

"Where's Colleen?" I had no sooner asked the question when my subconscious mind kicked in, and I heard the tremors of music coming from her room.

"Hi Harold, you're home early? Have a good day?" Carla turned to me and stopped abruptly. A carrot fell from her hand and hit the floor with a dull thud at her feet. Déjà vu.

"Are you ill? You look terrible, honey."

I ignored her and asked again. "Is Colleen in her room? With Pama?"

Carla frowned and bent to retrieve the carrot.

"Yes."

I turned towards the hallway when Carla asked, "Who's Pama?"

My mind didn't register her question. I was focused on Colleen's room.

I pounded on the door—the Piss Off sign flapping against it in time with the percussion of my fist. The music died.

Wait. Who's Pama?

"What?" An irritated voice that used to be so full of fondness for me answered.

Turning the handle, I pushed her door open. Colleen was sprawled on her bed, surrounded by schoolbooks. A big smile broke her face as she saw me.

"Oh, Hi, daddy."

What did she say? *Oh, hi, daddy?*

I stared at her, unsure. Something wasn't right. She should be angry with me. There was no sign of Pama. I glanced briefly around her room. God, I was so tired.

"Daddy? Are you okay?"

I brought my sore eyes back to hers.

"Where's Pama?"

Confusion creased her forehead as she sat on the edge of her bed. The book on her lap fell to the carpet. "Pama?"

"Yes, Pama. She spent the night with us. She went to school with you today. Your teacher adores her. In fact, the entire school just loves her. I've been, uh, sort of rude to her?"

Still no response.

"She has a tiny rattle around her neck on a chain."

Still that blank stare. What was going on?

"Who's Pama?" echoed in my ears. A wave of dizziness suddenly swept over me, and the room began to lose focus.

"Are you all right, Dad?"

"Where's Pama?" I braced myself and leaned into her room.

"I don't know any Pama, Daddy. Is that short for Pamela?" She looked frightened, not like she was hiding something, but she was beginning to be very afraid of me.

I stepped to her bed, my hands trembling.

"You don't know a Pama?"

Tears lined the bottoms of her mascara-lined eyes. Confusion and alarm poured into her eyes.

"No. Should I?"

I held her worried gaze for a moment longer, then gently touched her head's side. She didn't flinch. I hadn't been able to do that for a long time. She hadn't let me.

"No, honey, I'm sorry. I've had a terrible day. I think I need to get some sleep."

My feet headed for her bedroom door, my mind swirling with questions. I had lost touch with reality. Some switch inside my head had flipped to the off position, and I was staring down the long bleak tunnel of certain madness. It had to be. There was no other explanation.

"Daddy?"

"Um?" I turned to see my daughter rising from the bed. She was reaching for my hand. I looked down at her slim fingers, confused. We hadn't held hands since she was maybe nine years old. I hesitated and then enveloped her hand in mine. Our eyes met, and I saw something that had become a distant memory. Love. She looks just like a younger version of Carla. My heart ached.

"I love you, Daddy." She slid her arms around me and hugged me as we used to before life and stupidity had made us enemies. I held her close, almost afraid to let go because I knew this had to be a dream, a treacherously unfair dream. She let go, embarrassment suddenly flickering across her tear-streaked face.

I left her there, the warmth of her longed-for embrace sticking to my shirt like summer heat. She was worried about me. I was worried about me. Pama was real. She had to be. It was all too vivid, too intense, to be a dream. I stumbled into the kitchen. Carla was pulling a roast chicken out of the oven, its savoury fragrance teasing the gnawing teeth of hunger in my stomach. Chicken? Tonight? We don't have chicken on Wednesdays. Carla is like clockwork. I'm like clockwork. We always have lasagna mid-week, always.

What is going on?

"We're having chicken?" I asked numbly, my voice thin and distant sounding in my ears.

She turned to me, smiling warmly with just a hint of mischievousness.

"A change is as good as a move."

I just stared at her. She looked younger somehow. We hadn't changed our family traditions in years. Life was safer that way. Don't make any waves, don't get noticed, and the monsters won't find you that way. Or maybe, that was the delusion we had been living until Pama.

I would have asked Carla about Pama, but it seemed useless. I knew what the answer would be. *Who's Pama?* Had I been wrong about her, wrong about what she was, and why she had come into our lives?

In a fatigued daze, I stumbled out of the house. Carla called after me, but I ignored her. I saw her worried face in the rear-view mirror as I drove off. I needed to get to the mall where this indigestible nightmare had begun, back to where I had found the baby on the sidewalk.

I pulled into the mall parking lot and found a spot a few rows from the store entrance. I didn't lock the car; I don't think I even shut the door as I ran with a sudden renewed energy. I felt oddly expectant as I pushed past shoppers focused on their tasks. My left leg clipped a bumper, but the pain didn't register. My watch flashed 6:59 as I pushed past the last row of cars. I shot my gaze towards where I had found the baby the evening before.

Seven o'clock, Phyllis had said, every night near the main doors.

Pama wasn't there. What? I slumped in defeat. I thought for sure I had figured it out. Then suddenly, as if I had blinked, she was there, her one hand smashing the rattle repeatedly against the hard concrete, her other hand grinding the pebbles. Was she waiting for someone —for me?

Slowly, almost not breathing, I walked to her. Weariness raked my frame, but it had become just a distant, vague sensation.

Her near-naked body trembled with the anger I remembered from yesterday when I had first looked into her eyes. I knew that anger, and I knew that it came from my fear of what I could not control. I knew that feeling more surely than anything else in my life. I had no control over the frightening darkness of my closet or the shadows that danced across my bed from the tree outside my window. They were beyond my control, and I had vowed never to feel that way again in my young boy's brain. A carefully constructed life of order was the only way to cushion the fear that came from the inevitable uncertainties of life. It hadn't worked; chaos always found me, and so did the fear, my silent and unwelcome companion, squeezing my world smaller and smaller. I took few risks, not in life and not in love, and because I risked nothing, the wonder of living and the joy of loving was slipping through my fingers like sand.

I squatted in front of her and slowly reached for the hand that held the rattle. She lifted her curly head to mine, and our eyes met. Her dark eyes still shone with that strange maturity, but they no longer frightened me. On the contrary, I saw my release in them, just like I had seen my buried but desperate fear mirrored in them the day before.

"What the hell," I said, holding her close as I cast my gaze across the throng of ambivalent shoppers entering and leaving the grocery store.

Then I saw Phylis, the clerk with the bouncing blue ponytail, standing behind one of the store's large windows. She was looking at me and smiling.

I nodded and smiled back as I felt one of Pama's small hands gripping my shirt.

"Okay, let's take you home."

Note: Baby on the Sidewalk - This story is based on a dream as frantic and manic as you've just read. When it ended, I quickly got up and wrote it down, almost exactly as it is on these pages. I have many complex and sometimes bizarre dreams, but this one has haunted me for many years.

About the Author

Wyatt Tremblay is perhaps best known for his decades of political cartooning for the Yukon News. Born in Jasper, Alberta, he spent much of his life in the Yukon but now lives in  Airdrie, Alberta. His Christmas children's colouring book is available on iBooks. He is a regular arts feature writer for AirdrieLife Magazine.

Look for *Medusa Gone*, his first published novel by Raspberry Press, available on Amazon and elsewhere in print and digital.

Acknowledgements

I owe a great debt to those who have encouraged me to keep writing over the years and patiently listened as I regaled them with yet another crazy story from either my imagination or from a dream I'd had.

My siblings, children, friends, instructors, and strangers have contributed in various ways to this collection.

I must offer a heartfelt thank you to Josephine Holmes, who originally edited these words and who first helped me to believe I might be a writer, even though I had been feverishly scribbling my thoughts down on paper since I was 10.

Thank you also to Raspberry Press for being a friend to writers and helping make this book possible.

Finally, I wish to thank my best friend and partner in life, Bonnie, for believing in me.